Hot Tub Homicide

A Roseview Inn Cozy Mystery

Sally Bayless

e-book ISBN: 978-1-946034-39-7

Print ISBN: 978-1-946034-40-3

Kimberlin Belle Publishing LLC

Contact: admin@kimberlinbelle.com

Publisher's Note: This is a work of fiction. Names, characters, places, and incidents are a product of the author's imagination. Locales and public names are sometimes used for atmospheric purposes. Any resemblance to actual people, living or dead, or to businesses, companies, events, institutions, or locales is completely coincidental.

Cover art by DLR Cover Designs, www.dlrcoverdesigns.com.

Chapter One

"Why is a lawyer in Claremont, Missouri, writing to me?" I muttered to myself. I stared at the cream-colored envelope for a long moment, flipped through the rest of the mail, and closed the mailbox.

I must have stood there longer than I realized because seemingly from out of nowhere, a gust of wind ruffled my hair, a bolt of lightning split the sky, and rain began to pelt down.

I clutched the mail to my chest and sprinted for the door of my Kansas City ranch-style house.

Inside, I toed off my tennis shoes, dropped the mail on a side table, and padded into the kitchen, where I dried my face and hair with a kitchen towel.

Probably, unless I wanted my blond, chin-length hair to end up with all sorts of odd kinks from my natural curl, I should blow it dry.

Instead, I grabbed the mail, sat on the cozy blue couch, and pulled out that envelope from the lawyer's office.

How odd. Claremont was the little town in southern Missouri that I'd visited a month ago, back in April when I'd won three nights at a lakeside inn.

But why was a lawyer writing to me? With the way things had been going, I had to wonder if I was being sued for something I'd done while I was there.

After the spring I'd had, that was the last thing I needed.

Three months ago, the tech firm where I'd worked for four years had shut its doors without warning. Just like that, gone. I'd been the office manager—HR, event planning, glue-holding-the-team-together stuff—and I'd loved it. It was the first real purpose I'd found since my husband passed away. Losing the job felt like losing a second kind of stability.

Still, after a few weepy afternoons and that visit to Claremont, I'd dusted myself off. Updated my résumé. Rejoined LinkedIn. Told myself this could be a good thing. A fresh start. I actually believed it.

A few weeks later, within twenty-four hours, both of my best friends broke their own news. One's husband had landed a dream job in Minnesota. The other, who was my closest friend and a fellow widow, was moving to Arizona to help her newly divorced daughter raise the grandkids. Both of my friends felt terrible about the timing, but each one thought the other would still be here for me. Neither was.

Then the sad reality of my job hunt had sunk in. Getting hired to a new position at fifty-two wasn't that easy.

In fact, it wasn't easy at all.

Sometimes I wondered if my best days were behind me.

And now possibly more bad news. I looked down at the envelope from the firm of Blasington, Horkamp, and Wells. Thunder boomed outside as I sighed and slid a finger under the flap of the envelope. Then I unfolded the heavy stationery and drew in a shaky breath.

Dear Mrs. Whitfield,

I represent the estate of Mrs. Marjorie Everly, formerly of Claremont, Missouri.

You are named as a beneficiary in her will. At your earliest convenience, please contact me to discuss Mrs. Everly's bequest.

Cordially,

Jerome Blasington

My mouth went dry. Static filled my brain as I grabbed my cell phone from the end table and searched for the law firm online.

The firm, at least, looked real.

Just to be sure, I texted an old college friend who'd ended up a lawyer in Hannibal. Five minutes later, she texted back. Jerome Blasington was in good standing with the Missouri Bar. She included his phone number in the text, and it was the same one as in the letterhead.

I shot back a text of thanks and then I dialed, put the

phone on speaker, and set it on the couch cushion beside me.

After a brief time on hold, I reached Mr. Blasington.

"Mrs. Whitfield." His rich baritone voice came over the line. "I've been eagerly awaiting your call. Let me be the first to congratulate you on your inheritance."

"Uh, thank you," I replied, more than a little confused, "but I don't understand. I didn't know Marjorie Everly. Why would she leave me anything?"

"Do you remember visiting the Roseview Inn recently?"

"Yes, I won a prize to visit the inn about a month ago. I don't know for sure, but I think a former work colleague must have entered my name in a contest."

"I have to tell you, I advised Mrs. Everly that her ploy was not the right way to go about things. She should have called you and invited you directly, but she wanted to see your reaction when she told you about the inheritance. Unfortunately, she passed away a few days before your visit."

I blinked. "You mean, I didn't win a contest?"

"No. There was no contest. Just that letter about the 'prize' sent only to you."

I sank back into the couch cushions. I'd assumed a friend had entered my name without telling me. Instead, this poor woman had meant to surprise me and passed away before she had a chance. "I still don't know why she'd leave me anything..."

"Your husband was Clint Whitfield, born in Atchison, Kansas?"

"Yes. He died five years ago."

"Mrs. Everly was his great aunt. She said she met you once, right after you married, at a family reunion."

"Oh." I remembered going with Clint to a family reunion, but that had been thirty years ago. Even at the time, it had all been a blur. I'd met dozens of his relatives, including people we hadn't even invited to our small wedding.

"When Clint's cousin Archie died in February, Mrs. Everly revised her will. She said you weren't a blood relative but that she'd loved Clint when he was a boy."

"What exactly is the inheritance you're referring to?" Maybe it was a piece of family jewelry. Perhaps it might even be worth something.

"Oh, I should have explained sooner." The lawyer chuckled. "As soon as probate is completed, you'll be the owner of the Roseview Inn. Acreage, the historic building, all the contents, and the business."

My chest went hollow, and I opened my mouth, but no words came out.

"Please check your calendar and get back with me about when you'd like to come down. I normally wait longer to contact heirs, and it will take a few months to get probate wrapped up. However, since it's a small business currently in operation, I figured the sooner the better."

"So … I'll … I'll own the whole inn? After, uh, probate, I could move there and run the place?"

"If you so desire," Mr. Blasington said. "Or you could sell it. It's an attractive property. There's also a cat that belonged to Mrs. Everly. The staff are taking care of him, but I guess if you like him, he's yours as well." Papers rustled from his end of the phone line. "I'm sure you have a lot to think about. Please call my secretary to let her know when you'll be in town, and call me if you have any questions in the meantime."

"Thank you," I replied, stunned. Any questions? I had hundreds.

"Good day, Mrs. Whitfield."

"Good day."

The line disconnected, and I stared blankly across the room at a photo taken seventeen years ago of my sweet late husband, Clint, myself, and our only children, the twins when they were ten. If only Clint's car hadn't been hit by that semi and he were alive to hear this news.

I shook my head. "You always told me your family was full of surprises, sweetheart, but I never expected this."

For the next hour, I wandered about the house, feeling as if my brain were tingling. I changed out of my soggy shirt. I dried my hair. And I ate the supper I'd planned: pineapple chicken salad and a whole-wheat roll.

All in a state of shock.

By the time I put on my pajamas, the shock had faded, replaced by something I hadn't felt in weeks—the quiet flicker of hope. I pulled on my robe, took my suitcase down from the closet shelf, and set it by the bedroom door, ready for adventure.

Chapter Two

One week later, I woke at five in the morning, well before my alarm.

By six thirty, I'd loaded my last bag into the car, rechecked everything in the house, and slipped a key under my neighbor's doormat. Excitement bubbled up in my chest as I slid behind the wheel of my SUV, ready to drive to Claremont.

The day had warmed to about eighty by the time I arrived on the outskirts of town shortly before noon. Soon I spotted the sign for the inn, turned into the long driveway, and rounded a cluster of oak trees.

The Roseview Inn came into view at the top of the hill.

Tall and narrow, the historic structure was painted a cozy warm gray. It had three stories, white trim, and the classic slate Mansard roof of a Victorian in the Second Empire style. Gorgeous roses surrounded the building, which overlooked Lake Claremont. If I had to guess, I'd say almost every room had a view of the water.

Had it only been last Monday that I'd learned of my inheritance? Somehow, seeing it in real life made it even harder to believe.

The will was still going through probate, but for the next month, I'd be living at the inn and helping to run it. The setup was a bit unusual, but it would allow me to test out a possible new future for myself. With luck, I could even make myself useful.

According to the lawyer, the inn's two staff members, Kate Brooks and Addison Finch, had both agreed to stay on, pending my approval. I'd quickly given it. I'd met them both, as well as the inn's big orange cat, Tater, when I'd been here in April and liked them all.

Did I know for sure that I would keep the property after it officially became mine?

Well, no.

But for the next thirty-odd days, until mid-June, I was going to give life as the acting owner my best shot. With luck, the role might be my new job, something I definitely needed. Though I had a nephew named Sam who lived not too far away from here, over in Dogwood Springs, and was quite wealthy, my own finances were more pedestrian and required a regular paycheck.

I parked off to one side of the front lot, climbed out, and had just looked over at the tranquil lake below when I heard a bark, an angry *mrrrow*, and the rustle of leaves.

On the far side of the driveway, a German shepherd stood, front paws on a tree trunk, barking and leaping at—

"Oh, no!" I ran toward the dog, who had treed a large, pudgy orange tabby—Tater.

"You, hush!" I scolded the dog.

It immediately left the tree and turned to face me. It hung its head, but after a half-second, it cocked one ear and peeked up at me. It looked exactly like one of my twins used to when they were in trouble—wide-eyed, hoping cuteness would cancel any consequences.

It often worked for them, and it was equally effective for the German shepherd. What could I say? I was easily charmed.

"Are you friendly?" I asked.

The dog wagged its tail, and I stepped forward, holding out one hand.

It rushed over, sniffed my hand, and let me pet its soft fur.

"You really are a sweetie, aren't you?" I read the name on one of the dog's tags. "Marshall, huh? No wonder you're getting into trouble, Marshall. You look like you're not even a year old." He was a handsome young dog with bright eyes and shiny, well-brushed fur, clearly someone's much-loved pet.

From about six feet up the tree, the orange tabby hissed.

"Hmmm." I looked down at the dog. "I think you need to head home."

Marshall edged closer to me.

"Go home," I said firmly.

He lolled his head to one side and grinned at me.

"Marshall," I repeated, putting my hands on my hips. "Go home."

Understanding flashed in his eyes, and he turned and headed down a path toward the lake.

Good, one problem solved. Now, what to do about Tater? He was about a foot too high up the tree for me to reach him.

"Do you need help?" I stepped to the base of the tree and stretched my arms up toward him.

He blinked and glanced in the direction where the dog had disappeared. After a moment, he inched down.

I collected him and nestled him close to my chest. "Good job climbing down."

He nuzzled his fuzzy head against my chin.

I smiled. "I guess we're going to be housemates, aren't we?"

His purr vibrated against my chest, and I carried him to the inn, where a small sign on the front door invited guests to come in.

Tater was quite an armful, but for a second, I managed to hold him with one hand so I could use the other to open the door. Inside, I set him down.

He bounded away, and I looked around.

A twelve-foot ceiling rose above me, illuminated by a crystal chandelier, and a parquet floor spread beneath my feet.

Before me, an intricately carved wooden staircase led upstairs. A doorway to my left opened into a parlor filled with antique furniture and decorated in rich jewel tones. A matching doorway to my right led to a lobby with an antique mahogany bar counter serving as a reception desk.

Throughout it all, the smell of cheesy breakfast potatoes lingered.

"Welcome!" Addison Finch hurried over from the desk.

According to Mr. Blasington, Addison, who served as the inn's housekeeper and front desk clerk, was nineteen. She had long, wavy dark hair and intelligent brown eyes behind black-framed glasses.

"Addison, so nice to see you!" I said.

"You too." Her eyes shone. "Hold on," she added, pulling out her phone. "Let me tell Kate you're here."

A few seconds later, Kate Brooks, the inn's chef, dashed toward us.

Kate, who was in her late forties, had her red hair swept up in a clip and a smudge of what looked like chocolate batter on one sleeve—proof she'd come straight from the kitchen.

"Congratulations on your inheritance!" Kate said.

"Thank you." I smiled at her, but the doubt that had been in my mind as I drove down grew stronger.

Should I come out and say it? Yes. If I was going to make this my future, I needed to start out as honestly as possible.

"I feel rather awkward," I admitted. "I only met Mrs. Everly once, and that was thirty years ago. I keep thinking she could have left the inn to one of you."

Kate waved my words away. "Well, don't think that for another minute. Marjorie Everly was insistent that the inn stay in the family. The only other family she had left was a third cousin. He visited right before Christmas." She rolled her eyes.

"Talk about annoying," Addison muttered.

"Besides," Kate added, "Mrs. Everly didn't leave us out. She left me enough money to pay off the little house I took a mortgage out on two years ago."

"And me enough to pay for the rest of my degree in computer science," Addison said. "Even if I wanted to go away to school, which I don't." She twisted a plain gold band on her right hand. "I want to continue doing my degree online and stay here in Claremont, where I can look after my grandpa."

"So don't you worry one bit." Kate beamed at me. "We're both thrilled you're going to be the new owner, and we're hoping you like it well enough here to stay long-term."

"You're sure?"

They both nodded vigorously.

"So sure that Kate made lunch for us," Addison said.

A wave of happiness washed over me. I'd only walked in the door, and already I felt welcome.

"I almost forgot," I said. "A young German shepherd had chased Tater up a tree in the yard when I arrived. I told him to go home, and I brought Tater inside."

"I've seen that dog before," Kate said. "I think he belongs to the man renting the cottage that's on the next property over along the lake. I don't know the guy's name."

"Well, the dog's name is Marshall, according to his tag. I liked him, but Tater had no interest in being friends."

As if he'd heard his name, Tater strolled over and wound himself around my ankles.

"I think," Addison said, "that's Tater's way of saying 'thank you for rescuing me.'"

"My pleasure, Tater." I scratched his ears. "I think it's all part of my new job at the Roseview Inn."

The inn's two guests were out for the day, and the dining room didn't serve lunch to guests, so the three of us settled at a table there. Large windows overlooked the lake, and the sapphire-blue curtains and cream-and-gold wallpaper echoed the colors of the sky, clouds, and sun outside. Kate had made a flavorful quiche, yeasty home-made rolls, and a salad with orange-poppyseed dressing for lunch.

As we ate, I learned more about the operations of the inn. Before Mrs. Everly died, Kate had worked only in the kitchen. Mrs. Everly had primarily handled the front desk, and Addison had done laundry and housekeeping. After Mrs. Everly's death five weeks ago, Kate and Addison had been scrambling, trying to keep the place running.

"Even if you're new to working at an inn, you'll at least be another person to pitch in," Addison said.

"I'll do all I can to help," I promised, and I sat up taller. This might not turn out to be the right path forward for me, but for the time being, I was needed.

We planned a more in-depth discussion for the next day,

then I carried in my things and took the key Addison gave me to the owner's second-floor suite.

Tater followed along the hall as I rolled my suitcase toward the unmarked door at the back of the building and let myself in.

I was eager to talk to Addison and learn more about running the front desk, but I took a quick look around.

The suite was maybe eight hundred square feet. A bedroom, a small sitting room, a bath, and a galley-style kitchen with a tiny table for two. It was decorated much like the inn, in rich jewel tones and antiques.

In here, though, the antiques seemed more delicate and valuable. They were also more crowded in, with every flat surface except the kitchen table covered in glass and pottery. I spotted a pink Fenton bowl with a ruffled edge, a vase I thought might be Rookwood, and a stunning cut-glass biscuit jar. Individually, the pieces were delightful, but together it felt like too much, as if Mrs. Everly had been reluctant to part with any of her treasures.

Tater hopped up on the couch as if accustomed to having the run of the place. I found his food and water bowls in the kitchen, a bag of dry cat food under the sink, and his litter box in a utility room. A cat door in the bottom of the door to the suite ensured he could come and go as he pleased.

In the bedroom, two cardboard boxes sat in the corner, each labeled "Dresser/Clothing." A third held the items from the top of the dresser and the bathroom. In the closet, clothes had been shoved to one side and a dozen empty hangers filled the middle of the rod.

If I stayed, there would be a lot to sort out. I loved the antiques, but my decorating comfort zone was "less is more." Too much stuff around me made me jittery. If everything worked out in probate and I moved permanently to the Roseview Inn, perhaps I could sell some of the antiques from the owner's suite to fund improvements to the property. A building this old had to be in frequent need of repairs.

For today, though, the space was certainly livable.

I unpacked my suitcase, opened the door to the hall, and asked Tater if he'd like to come with me.

He was fast asleep on the couch, so I left him there and returned to the front desk.

Addison began my unofficial orientation with a full tour of the property, starting with the first floor. In addition to the lobby and the parlor, the public space on the first floor included the dining room and a large library with cozy chairs perfect for curling up to read. The library could be connected through double doors to the dining room, making one huge room that spanned the width of the building. In the back of the first floor were the kitchen, a powder room, the laundry room, a single ADA-accessible suite, and what had been the servants' staircase. A first-floor litter box for Tater was tucked in that back staircase.

In addition, near the laundry room was the original dumbwaiter, which worked on a series of pulleys. Addison said the ropes had been replaced and that they still used the dumbwaiter to transport linens up and down stairs.

"Tater's allowed everywhere," she added, "except the dining room and kitchen. As you may remember, guests can let him visit in their rooms if they like."

"The second floor," she said as she led me up the stairs, "has your owner's quarters, two suites, and one regular room. "The third floor has six regular rooms. With the ADA room, that makes ten rooms total."

After touring the third floor, we went back downstairs to the library, out a set of double doors, and down a path to a large patio. Off to one side, behind a row of boxwoods, were an in-ground hot tub and a large fire pit.

"From here," Addison said, indicating two small signs, "that path leads to Lookout Point, which has the best view of the lake, and this one goes to a small dock and storage shed by the water. This one"—she pointed to a narrower, unmarked path—"goes to the staff fire pit."

I nodded. Our tour finished outside a large carriage house. It looked charming from the outside, but Addison said it needed work and was only used for storage.

Then she gave me my first lesson in managing the inn: how to check in a guest and prepare their bill at checkout.

The system was all on paper and seemed rather archaic, but I soon began to get the hang of it. The more I settled into the front desk process, though, the more I thought about the five weeks since Mrs. Everly had passed away.

"Addison." I turned to her. "When's the last time you had a full day off?"

"Tax Day, which was Mrs. Everly's funeral." She straightened a pile of guest information folders on the reception desk. "We closed and even canceled a reservation."

"April fifteenth?" I took a step back. "That's more than a month ago and hardly a day to relax if you attended a funeral."

"Even if Kate watched the desk, someone had to stay here overnight, and she's got an elderly dog at home, so I did it. I live with my grandpa, but everything was okay as long as I could spend some time at home with him each day."

"Go home." I waved her toward the door. "You already gave me your cell number. I'll call if there's a crisis."

"But I—you—"

"There are only two guests in the inn. I can man the desk from three until six, regular check-in hours in case someone unexpected arrives, and handle anything that comes up overnight. I've already found all I need to take care of Tater, who's my responsibility now. You can train me more on running the inn in the morning."

"Are you sure?" Uncertainty crossed her face.

"Completely sure."

Her eyes widened, and her shoulders eased. "Sheesh. That would be epic."

She showed me the sign she set out with her phone number when the desk was closed. I assured her that I could make a similar temporary sign with my own number and waved goodbye.

She practically skipped out the door.

I felt rather happy myself. I'd always loved helping people, and while innkeeping was mostly about serving guests, it felt good to help Addison as well. She'd clearly been carrying too much for too long.

I made a mental note to check whether she and Kate had been paid overtime, then settled down behind the desk, ready for my first few hours on the job. Tater appeared from the library, hopped up on the desk, and settled near me to give himself a bath. The inn was nearly silent, and I exhaled slowly, tension melting from my shoulders. Maybe I'd been more nervous about this one-month trial than I'd realized.

After all, it had come after a really difficult period in my life.

Most people might have found it strange how much the job I'd lost had meant to me. Everyone else there had been at least twenty years younger than me, and my role hadn't been one of the glamorous jobs in the company.

But I'd felt important. I'd felt appreciated for the way I anticipated needs and remembered the little things like favorite snacks. I'd set up weekly team-building picnics, carry-in chili cookoffs, and pizza parties that let others connect and find joy in their workplace. Plus, I'd been the one people had come to when they needed help navigating the more difficult personalities on the team.

All that sense of self-worth had disappeared overnight.

Before I'd even caught my breath, everyone else was moving on, snapped up by other local tech firms or hired to out-of-town jobs their buddies from college had helped them secure.

Suddenly, I'd felt old. Out of place. Like my best days were over.

Then there'd been the pain of watching my two best friends move away. They'd been the women I leaned on for emotional support, for silliness to make me laugh, for the special kind of caring that only other women can bring. Oh, they'd done their best to stay in touch, but we all knew that new people would soon fill the gaps in their days. I would become less and less a part of their lives.

So, finding a new job—here at the inn or back in Kansas City—wasn't only about income. It was about finding a new ... me.

I sighed and settled down behind the desk, looking over all Addison had taught me.

After about half an hour, the man staying in Room 8 stopped at the desk to ask for more towels, and I was able to find them with no problem.

We discussed how lovely the lake looked, and he told me how he preferred staying at the Roseview Inn, located on Lake Claremont—the quiet lake where no speedboats were allowed—compared to the hotels at nearby Bellamy Lake— the loud, raucous, party lake. Eventually, he headed upstairs.

I sat back down with a smile. Running an inn was almost like hosting a houseguest, and it seemed rather surreal that this could earn money. I didn't want to get ahead of myself, but maybe this was the right spot for me. Maybe life at the inn would work out just fine.

Really, how hard could it be?

Chapter Three

THE NEXT MORNING, I eagerly began to check out my first guest.

Unfortunately, she'd overslept and was upset that there wasn't a bagged breakfast she could take with her while driving. I tried to explain that the inn offered a delicious sit-down breakfast and even remembered that the day's menu was made-to-order omelets and homemade biscuits and gravy.

She didn't care.

She was even more irritated when I struggled with her credit card and Tater circled her legs, leaving orange fur clinging to her black pants.

"Let me help," Addison said as soon as she walked in.

She pulled a lint roller from a desk drawer and handed it to the woman. She made a quick call to Kate, who brought out a to-go coffee and a sausage-and-egg biscuit wrapped in wax paper. Then, in less than a minute, Addison had taken care of the billing and booked a room for the woman's return trip.

"You need someone at the desk who knows what they're doing," the woman muttered. She took a sip of coffee and stood up taller, then gave Tater a pat on the head and walked out the door.

"Oh, Addison, thank you," I said. "I guess I still have a lot to learn."

"You'll figure it out," Addison replied. "She stays here a lot, and she's normally not that grumpy."

"I think she just needed caffeine," Kate said.

"Maybe." Or maybe I'd been totally clueless.

Drat. I wasn't sure I wanted to run an inn, but I didn't want to lose the option just because I was a disaster at it.

I reminded myself that I hadn't even been here twenty-four hours. I certainly wasn't giving up yet.

As luck would have it, the inn had no reservations for the night. Ordinarily, that would be a bad thing, but it did give me more time to get my bearings. "Ready to sit down and discuss the inn in more detail?" I asked Kate and Addison.

"Ready," they said in unison, but their reply didn't sound like a resounding chorus. Instead, it sounded more like a chant of dread.

A twist of tension shot through my stomach.

Two hours later, I sat back in my chair in the dining room and thought about what I'd learned.

Kate had worked in hospitality for two decades. At the height of her career, she'd catered huge, high-end special events in St. Louis. Two years ago, she'd moved back to Claremont, her hometown, and taken a step down in her career to serve as the head chef for the inn's breakfast and afternoon tea so she could recover from burnout. According to Addison, when Mrs. Everly had hired Kate, it had been a huge win for the inn. Kate's appetizers were delicious, and the miniature desserts she offered at teatime were so good that some guests claimed they stayed at the inn simply to have a chance to eat them.

Addison might be young, but she was highly intelligent and in her second year of earning a degree in computer science. Like Kate, she was deeply dedicated to the inn.

With decent occupancy, they said, the inn should be quite profitable. The roof and HVAC system were good. The plumbing had been redone ten years ago when the bathroom in each room had been redecorated in an elegant, classic style. The lake, of course, was gorgeous.

Beyond that, the news hadn't been good. Occupancy, which needed to average six of the ten rooms filled every night for the inn to be profitable, was far too low. Even in the peak season of summer, the inn had nights completely empty.

I turned back to face them. "So, basically, you're saying that the inn is surviving—barely—because of overflow guests from hotels at Bellamy Lake and a handful of guests who've been coming here for years?"

Addison's eyes tensed, and she looked at Kate, but for at least a minute, neither said a word.

Then Kate leaned in, hands spread out on the table. "There's a lot that could be done."

"We tried to convince Mrs. Everly to move past 1980," Addison said. "She always made you believe she might change, but she never did."

"I think," Kate said, "she was happier in the past, and she not only wanted to respect it, but cling to it." She shook her head. "It didn't always help the inn."

"What would you all recommend?" I asked.

In an instant, their body language changed, as if my question hadn't been what they expected. Suddenly, they both spoke at once, ideas tumbling out. Addison even volunteered to help with any tech issues, saying she loved new projects.

I listened and carefully made a list of their suggestions: an updated website with online booking, a web presence with online travel agents and consolidated booking, modern marketing techniques, and improved Wi-Fi. Most importantly—based on guest complaints—larger beds with no footboards, the bane of tall travelers. Because of Mrs. Everly's insistence on preserving the historic atmosphere, all the rooms contained double beds in antique frames. There wasn't room in the regular rooms for two queens, but each could easily hold a king.

I tapped the printouts Addison had given me—a logical, well-organized summary of the inn's occupancy rates, income, and expenses. "From what you're telling me, the inn can't stay open much longer if things continue the way they are."

"Probably not," Kate said, frowning.

"I appreciate you pulling this information together, Addison. And thank you both for being honest with me and offering your ideas. Unfortunately, until probate is settled, I don't have the power to spend the money to make changes this big without Mr. Blasington's approval."

Addison's face fell, and Kate's mouth thinned into a line.

I tapped my pen on the table. "On the other hand, I don't want to sit around watching things get worse." I drew in a deep breath and squared my shoulders. "I think our best hope is to prepare solid evidence to present to Mr. Blasington, evidence that these changes are in the best interest of the inn. I'll start on some research this afternoon."

Kate's smile returned, and Addison volunteered to help.

"Are you sure?" I looked over at her. "I was thinking you could give me another hour of training and take the rest of the day off."

"If we don't make changes right now, the inn will close," Addison said. "And I'm good online."

"I bet you are," I agreed. "If you're offering help, I'll take it."

For the next three days, in between Addison giving me hands-on lessons in taking care of our few guests, she and I gathered information. We read online. I downloaded a few e-books about running an inn. I even called a high school friend who had traveled so widely that she'd visited all seven continents and spent three hours on the phone with her.

At last, I made an early afternoon appointment to talk with Mr. Blasington.

The minute it was over, I drove back to the inn and sat down with Addison and Kate, once again in the empty dining room.

"First of all"—I slid checks across the table toward each of them—"I insisted he write checks to pay for all the overtime you've put in."

Kate quickly thanked me, but Addison looked down at hers, which was a considerable amount, and her eyes grew huge. "You didn't need to do this, Meredith."

"I did, and Mr. Blasington apologized. He said he never even thought about the operations of the inn. He didn't realize Mrs. Everly had taken such an active role."

Kate patted Addison's arm. "The inn would have closed without what you did."

"Thank you." Addison carefully folded the check in half, in half again, and slid it in her back pocket.

"And..." I looked at Addison, then Kate. "He agreed to us spending some of the inn's limited capital for our plan."

"What part?" Kate asked.

I grinned. "Every. Single. Thing."

They let out whoops of delight.

"First," I said, "we hire Addison as a consultant to set up a fully featured website with online reservations—something we can access from the desk or our phones. She will be paid a fair rate as a computer science consultant—not a housekeeper's wage."

Addison murmured that the pay upgrade wasn't necessary, but Kate and I disagreed.

"Second, a Wi-Fi upgrade and USB outlets in all the rooms," I continued. "Restful and quiet are wonderful, but people need an option if they can't, or don't want to, unplug. Third, we buy king-size mattresses and high-quality bedding, and we have custom padded headboards made with vinyl covering for easy cleaning."

I pulled out a sketch I'd made. "You can easily buy padded vinyl headboards that look modern, but we need a curvy shape that looks Victorian. I don't know who we're going to get to make these, but there has to be somebody."

"Ooh, I like the looks of that." Kate tapped my sketch. "Plus, I know someone who could do the work. She's a retired teacher who loves woodworking and crafts."

"That would be wonderful." I beamed at her. "The final change I recommended was that we raise rates by fifteen percent immediately."

"That's been needed for a while," Kate said.

"He really agreed to it all?" Addison said.

"Every bit. He said the changes served the estate's best interest and authorized us to spend the money."

"Fabulous!" Kate's eyes sparkled. "I can't believe how encouraged I feel. I know what I'm going to do to celebrate."

"What?" Addison and I both asked.

"I'm going to plan a reception for local business owners. They need to know that the Roseview Inn will be an even better place to send tourists, and you, Meredith, need a chance to meet them."

A reception? I blinked, my brain still partly celebrating the lawyer's approval. "I don't know for sure that I'm staying."

Yes, I knew I wanted to do the best for the inn in the short term. Yes, I felt as if we were becoming a team. And yes, I wanted to stay. But wanting wasn't the same as deciding. What if I wasn't good at it? What if, after a week, I hated it?

I wasn't ready to commit.

"How are you going to know for sure that you want to stay here if the only locals you meet are the two of us?" Kate gestured to Addison and herself. "You all focus on the upgrades and leave the reception to me. It's going to be an event at the Roseview Inn that no one will ever forget."

I looked at her and Addison, both beaming at me.

After a second, I slowly nodded.

"Let's do it," I said. "An event at the Roseview Inn that no one will ever forget."

Chapter Four

SINCE THE INN had no guests the next morning, I took advantage of the freedom to sleep in a bit, gave Tater food and water, then headed out for a stroll. No matter the temperature—rain or shine or snow—I loved walking outside. Today, when it was sunny and just warm enough that I didn't need a jacket, I couldn't wait to begin.

I took the path to Lookout Point and sat on a bench near the bluff's edge. I gazed out over the marina and the heart of Claremont along the shore to the west, a scattering of homes peeking out from the trees along the rest of the visible shore, and acres of blue water. A soft breeze caressed my skin and rustled the leaves. A bird that I thought was a blue heron emerged from the reeds in a nearby cove and flew around the bend and out of sight. A palpable peace and tranquility settled over me. I might not end up keeping the inn, but for now, the opportunity to spend this time in nature was a gift I didn't want to take for granted.

Finally, my heart full, I returned to the back patio and took the path down to the lake for a walk along the shore. I stood on the small wooden dock a moment and then headed east, away from town, my mind full of ideas about the inn.

Yesterday, Kate, Addison, and I had made a plan.

Kate had reached out to the teacher she knew, who was delighted with the headboard project and promised a reasonable rate. Addison would come up with suggestions for the website and Wi-Fi and discuss them with Kate and me. I would find sources for king-size mattresses, bedding, and vinyl, and I'd order samples of the vinyl so I could pick the best patterns.

In addition, tonight we had three rooms filled and I'd get more practice with the day-to-day tasks of being an innkeeper. With luck, I'd manage not to—

"Marshall! Get back here!" A man's voice rang out.

There was a rustling in the underbrush up the hill and the sound of someone running.

As I neared a narrow trail that led uphill from the lake, I spotted a small white cottage nestled among the trees at the top of the rise. A few seconds later, a familiar-looking German shepherd burst through the underbrush carrying a tennis shoe in his mouth.

Covered in burrs, he raced over in front of me, dropped the shoe at my feet, and lolled his head to one side.

"Well, hello there." I bent down to pick up the shoe. It looked brand new, and except for some slobber on the toe area that I avoided touching, no worse for wear.

"Marshall, bring that back!" A man came out from behind the trees, jogging awkwardly. He looked to be about my age with brown hair, a hint of a beard, and glasses.

"Um, hi." He glanced down at the shoe I held.

He was wearing the mate, and his other foot was bare.

I smiled and held out the shoe. "This looks like it's yours."

"Thank you." His ears turned slightly pink, and he bent down to put it on.

Marshall hurried to his side and sat down, looking for all the world like he expected a treat for providing the man with some exercise.

The man gave him a look of loving exasperation and reached out to shake my hand. "I'm Philip Holt." He gestured to the dog. "This miscreant is my dog, Marshall."

I shook his hand. "I'm Meredith Whitfield. As soon as things work through probate, I'll be the owner of the Rose-view Inn."

Philip looked impressed.

"A relative of my late husband left it to me. It was quite unexpected." I gave Marshall a pat. "Good to see you again," I said to him.

Philip's brow creased. "You've met Marshall before?"

"Two days ago." I chuckled. The dog had certainly added excitement to my arrival.

"Uh-oh," Philip said. "What did he do?"

As gently as I could, trying not to get Marshall in too much trouble, I explained how he had treed Tater.

Philip looked mortified.

"When I told him to stop, he did immediately, and he came right over and was really sweet. And when I told him to go home, he headed this direction."

Philip gave a wry grin. "That was the morning he learned how to open the screen door by nudging the handle. I had no idea he'd caused so much trouble."

"Well, no harm was done. Tater wasn't hurt, and he didn't seem that scared, merely offended."

"I'm keeping the screen door latched now that I'm onto that trick," Philip said. "Marshall is smart, but he's not at the top of his class in obedience school."

"I doubt Tater would put up with obedience school," I replied. "He's a darling, but I've always been of the opinion that cats train the humans, not the other way around."

Philip laughed, and his brown eyes twinkled. "You make a good point. Are you new to Claremont?"

I nodded.

"I'm fairly new myself. I'm a history professor from up in Columbia, here for a year on sabbatical to write a book about early lead mine owners in the area, including the man who built the house that eventually became the Rose-view Inn."

"Ooh, I'd love to learn more about the inn's history, and I'd be happy to give you a tour sometime if you'd like to see the place."

"I'd really appreciate that!" He scratched Marshall's ears. "And you can tell Tater that Marshall will stay home."

"Probably for the best," I agreed with a grin.

"C'mon, Marshall," Philip said. "We need to go home

and brush out those burrs you managed to get into." He waved at me and headed up the path to his cottage.

Marshall trotted along beside him, happy as could be.

I turned back toward the inn, ready to begin the hunt for king-size mattresses that were high quality, comfortable, and reasonably priced.

Philip Holt...

I smiled. I had a feeling I'd enjoy talking with him and learning more of the inn's history.

Over Memorial Day weekend, the inn was packed, and I learned just how much laundry full occupancy entailed. Once the weekend passed, though, the place emptied out.

The following Thursday evening, we had no guests for the night, and the reception Kate had planned was in full swing. About a dozen local business owners milled around the library with some wandering through its double doors and down the path to the patio.

Although it had been hot earlier in the day, the temperature outside was perfectly balmy, and the lake below us looked beautiful. Over near the hot tub, a fire burned in the big guest fire pit in case anyone wanted to sit around it once the sun set.

Kate kept the buffet in the library filled with appetizers, soft drinks, wine, and tropical cocktails.

Addison bounced between chatting with people and hovering at my side, where she intentionally used the business owners' names in conversation, helping me remember who was who.

I'd greeted everyone as they came in and was moving from one cluster of people under the shade of an umbrella to another on the patio, joining conversations, and trying to be a good hostess.

I paused for a rather loud drum solo on the Beach Boys playlist, then turned my attention back to a conversation with Rita Alder and Lena Quinn. Rita was a plump, cheerful blond woman in her early sixties who ran Claremont Gifts. Lena was Kate's quieter younger sister, a librarian with long auburn hair.

"I'm going to pop back in and get another of these delicious cheese puffs Kate made." I took a half-step toward the door. "Can I refresh a drink for either of you?"

"That would be great." Rita handed me her glass. "Diet soda, if you don't mind."

"Happy to help." I had a spring in my step as I walked toward the path to the library, listening to "Surfin' U.S.A.," and mentally reviewing the names of people as I passed.

That good-looking guy with dark hair and a carefully trimmed beard was Tony Rossini, the owner of Bellamy Pointe, an upscale hotel on Bellamy Lake. Tony was in his late forties and struck me as a bit pompous—but smart, capable, and charming.

He was both the competition and one of our greatest sources of guests, as Bellamy Pointe sent the inn its overflow.

The man beside him, J.B. Hodges, ran J.B.'s Steak &

Seafood. He was about the same age as Tony, but blond and more muscular, with a guarded air that left me unable to tell for sure if I liked him.

I could definitely tell, though, that there was tension between him and Tony. As I drew near, J.B. took a long swig of his drink and shot Tony a smirk. Tony's jaw tightened.

Holy cow, I hoped the reception wouldn't be marred by a testosterone-induced scuffle.

Luckily, Tony spun around and strode over to talk to Shannon Lenox.

Shannon, the youngest of the business owners, was an attractive woman in her thirties with light-brown hair, blue eyes, and dimples that brightened her whole face. She ran Shannon's Bookshop, which also served tea and coffee.

The only other people on the patio were Vanessa Moran, a local real estate agent who appeared to be in her mid-forties but was trying hard to look younger, and Elliot Renner, a rather pretentious art gallery owner. Vanessa had dark-blond hair and wore high-heeled sandals that looked painful. Elliot was in his late fifties, had ears that seemed too large for his head, and reminded me of a nervous, long-legged water bird.

I overheard Vanessa talking about the difficulties of working on her own, and Elliot sympathizing.

I gave them my warmest hostess smile as I passed. "Just getting Rita a refill, and then I'm eager to talk with both of you."

They nodded, and I slipped inside.

Once my eyes adjusted to being out of the sunshine, I

spotted the rest of the business owners chatting. The woman who owned the marina, the guy who ran the bike shop, and the ice cream parlor owner were all offering congratulations to a smiling bald man, who'd recently married the gentleman who was his business partner in running the gourmet grocery store.

At the top of the staircase, settled into position like a loaf-shaped emperor, Tater peered down at the reception.

I gave him a little wave and hurried over to the buffet, where someone had spilled red wine on the stack of paper napkins. I cleaned up the mess and hurried back into the kitchen to hunt down more.

With that problem solved, I ate a cheese puff, set another on my plate, and pulled the diet soda bottle from where it had been relegated behind the wine. I bent down, struggling to unscrew the cap and—

A blood-curdling scream came from the patio.

I jerked upright and dashed outside, appetizers and drinks forgotten.

"Help! Over here!" The cry came from near the in-ground hot tub.

I rounded the boxwoods and found Lena bending over the edge of the hot tub, trying to pull J.B. out. "He's not moving," she yelled.

Good grief! How many cocktails had J.B. drunk? I hurried closer.

Tony rushed past me from the main patio, kicked off his loafers, and pulled J.B. out of the hot tub. He and Lena positioned J.B. on his side, and Tony slapped him hard on the back. "C'mon, buddy, cough up the water and come to."

J.B. didn't respond.

A plastic cocktail cup bobbed in the water, spinning lazily in the ripples from Tony's movements. A maraschino cherry floated beside it, and a phone lay in the bottom of the water.

I reached for my own phone, unlocking it to call 911.

"Kate's already calling for help," Addison said, appearing beside me.

I looked again at J.B. and darted forward to touch Tony's arm. "He's not just—I mean—look." I pointed.

A raw wound on the back of his head parted J.B.'s wet hair.

"I see it, but first things first," Tony replied. "We've got to do CPR."

Lena backed away, and Vanessa rushed to J.B.'s side. She and Tony, who both seemed to know what they were doing, began chest compressions.

Nausea swirled in my stomach. Maybe it was the smell of the hot tub chemicals or the chaos around me or simply the fact that Kate had worked so hard setting up this reception for me to meet local business owners, but now...

Well, it could be that J.B. had gotten drunk, fallen in a way that he hit his head, and ended up in the water. I pictured him walking backward, tripping over his own feet perhaps, and falling in and hitting his head on the concrete side of the hot tub. That would explain the wound on the back of his head.

But then how did he end up face down in the water? After the head injury, he could have stumbled about the water and fallen in face forward, but it seemed unlikely. If he'd been conscious after he hit his head, he would have climbed out or called for help.

I wanted to believe the whole thing was a terrible, tragic accident, but something about it didn't sit right in my mind.

Maybe ... it wasn't an accident.

Chapter Five

Sirens drew closer, and a couple of minutes later, three paramedics rushed onto the patio.

Two of them quickly took over CPR from Tony and Vanessa. The other urged us back, then went over to help her colleagues.

I sat down with Addison at one of the patio tables, realizing after I sank into the chair how shaky I was. For a long moment, I only seemed capable of focusing on a bird who was singing happily, unaware of the tragedy, and the long shadows created by the sun, now low in the sky.

Eventually, I felt steadier, and I looked around.

The people who had been in the library had come outside and stuck together. The marina owner, the bike shop guy, the ice cream lady, and the bald guy from the gourmet grocery store stood clustered by a table. They looked concerned, whispering to one another, but overall composed.

The others—the ones who'd been outside—were scattered across the patio. They looked far less calm.

I thought back to that wound on J.B.'s head, and unease welled inside me. If what happened to him wasn't an accident, if someone had attacked J.B., one of them was probably the culprit. My mouth went dry.

That attack was probably done by only one person, though. The rest of these people were innocent and were here as my guests. I had a responsibility to help them if I could, especially anyone who seemed distressed.

I scanned the patio.

Kate's sister Lena, who had been the first to try to rescue J.B., had backed far from the hot tub near a row of lounge chairs and was trembling. Kate was with her and had grabbed a towel, which she was wrapping around her. Since it was still in the low eighties, Lena's reaction was probably more from shock than cold. Realizing Kate could comfort her sister better than I could, I turned to the other guests.

Rita, the gift shop owner, looked unfazed, arms folded over her chest. Beside her, Shannon's jaw was tight, but her eyes shone with unshed tears.

Tony and Vanessa stood together, and Tony was muttering about wanting to get home and put on dry clothes. Both seemed eager to leave.

Elliot, pale and wide-eyed, stood all alone. Of all the people on the patio, perhaps he needed emotional support the most.

I nudged Addison. "Let's go talk to Elliot."

Just as we got to our feet, two of the paramedics loaded J.B. into the ambulance.

A half-second later, a tall man in his mid-thirties rounded the corner of the inn. "Detective Cal Granger, here for the Claremont Police," he announced, although everyone seemed to recognize him.

He ran a hand through his short brown hair and walked over to the paramedic who was still outside the ambulance.

A hush fell over the patio as we all strained to hear what the detective said.

Luckily, he made no attempt to lower his voice. "Wound on the back of the head? And the body was found face down in the water?" His words rang with suspicion, and his gray eyes narrowed as he scanned all of us.

The paramedic murmured something I couldn't hear, but the look on his face made it clear that he didn't think the rescue attempt was going to end well.

The detective pulled out his phone and spoke into it. "I need a crime scene team over here, ASAP, and as many officers as you can spare."

Then he turned to face the people on the patio. "Folks, I'm going to need everyone to take a seat and refrain from talking to each other. This is now an active crime scene."

A murmur rippled through the crowd, and a chill prickled down my spine. So, it wasn't just me. The police suspected something too.

The detective cleared his throat. "I've got backup coming. Once they arrive, we'll need to interview each of you."

I glanced at Addison, and we sat back down. I shot a sympathetic look at Elliot and angled my head toward the empty seat next to me. He shuffled over and slumped into it. Now that Cal had made it clear he didn't believe what happened to J.B. was an accident, Elliot looked even paler and more frightened.

Frightened pretty much covered it for me as well, especially when the detective later told us that J.B. did not survive.

Because with what I'd seen and the way Detective Granger was acting, it seemed almost certain that J.B. had been murdered.

I let out a shaky sigh.

Murder—not an accident.

Not the welcome to Claremont I'd been hoping for.

The next afternoon, Addison and I sat behind the desk in the lobby staring at the new laptop she had ordered and set up.

"So that's the new website and online booking system," she said. "It's all ready for someone to use it."

"That's fantastic, Addison."

"Not a big deal. Just helping out," she said, her cheeks turning pink.

"No, it *is* a big deal. It's key to the inn's survival."

She'd done an amazing job, but I couldn't manage to make my voice sound as appreciative as I'd like. And even though I'd finalized the decision on the bedding to order, I hadn't made any purchases.

Yesterday at this time, everything had been working well, and my fresh start in Claremont had seemed like a great idea. Today, with the patio marked off with crime scene tape and the prospect looming of later having to drain and clean the hot tub where J.B. had died, the thought of selling the inn and finding a job in Kansas City sounded much more appealing.

Addison looked over at me and let out a long sigh.

Apparently, it wasn't just me who felt as if our wonderful plans to rejuvenate the inn didn't matter anymore.

Only Tater, lounging in a sunbeam near the windows, seemed himself.

"That idiot!" Kate stomped through the library toward us. Her blue eyes were dark, and her breathing came heavy.

"What's wrong?" I asked as Addison and I rushed toward her.

"Cal Granger took Lena in for questioning! My baby sister! I swear he doesn't have any more sense now than he did when I babysat him when he was little!" She jammed her hands onto her hips and rolled her eyes.

"Can't they talk to people and develop some sort of a timeline?" I asked. "Like J.B. was talking with this person and then was seen walking away with them and not seen again?"

"Apparently not," Kate said. "Nobody was really paying attention. They were all milling around, talking to one person and then the next. And some people walked over to get a better view of the lake. With the boxwood hedge near the hot tub and fire pit and the clusters of trees blocking the view, the patio's not all visible at once."

I supposed that made sense. If that was the case, the police would have to rely more on physical evidence and motive. "Why would Lena want to kill J.B.?"

Addison nudged my elbow. "Um, until recently, they were a thing. The breakup was rather ugly and public."

Oh. "Lots of people have breakups, though. They don't end in murder."

"Cal says she has motive," Kate said, "and he heard she was yelling at him at a local bar a couple of weeks ago."

"Lena isn't the yelling type," Addison said softly.

"That's what you'd think if you didn't grow up with her," Kate said. "She's quiet and mild-mannered, but only up to a point. When she loses it, she really loses it."

I'd known people like that.

"He also says she found the body," Kate said. "I guess that's something killers sometimes do—act like they found the victim so that if their DNA is on the body, they have an excuse."

"It does make sense," Addison said slowly. "Although I can't in a million years imagine Lena as a killer."

"Of course not!" Kate agreed. "But I don't think Cal's even considering anyone else as a suspect. I wish somebody could get him to see reason."

Her words hung in the air, and my chest grew tight.

Sure, when I'd been here in April, I'd helped figure out

who committed a crime at the inn, but that had been something much less serious—not a murder. And unlike then, this time Cal Granger recognized that a crime had taken place and was supposedly working to find the killer.

Kate's phone rang, startling the three of us.

"It's my mom." Kate answered the call and walked away toward the kitchen, talking as she went. From what we could hear, it sounded as if her mom was even angrier than she was.

"Oh." Addison glanced at her phone, then stood up quickly. "It's time for me to take Grandpa to his meeting."

Her grandfather, a man in his eighties who had been a local jeweler, had been a key member of a local service organization for decades. She'd told me he was being honored by the group for fifty years of service, and she was invited to attend.

"Have a good time," I called as she dashed out the door.

While I sat alone in the lobby, I thought about how sweet Lena had seemed. Time seemed to drag as I waited for our guests for the evening to check in, a couple staying in one of the suites.

I'd carefully considered how I'd tell our guests about the murder. The police had finished collecting evidence and assured me the inn was safe. Still, I wanted to be upfront with guests. I had called each reservation for the next week, explained the situation, and offered them a choice. Either I would cancel their reservation, or I would offer a coupon to a local restaurant for dinner. The couple tonight had opted for the free dinner, but half of the guests canceled.

How long until the murder dried up our current trickle of guests completely? It sure would be better for the inn if this mess was resolved.

My shoulders sank. I didn't want that resolution to mean Kate's sister being charged with murder. She'd seemed so nice, chatting about her favorite books to read aloud to preschoolers. I didn't think she was a killer.

Something soft and fuzzy nuzzled my ankle.

I looked down and found Tater rubbing his cheek against my leg, right below the hem of my cropped pants.

"Oh, hello, big fella." I reached down and scratched the base of his ears.

He gazed up at me with his huge green eyes and hopped up into my lap. Then he nuzzled my shoulder and settled down, purring loudly. A bittersweet ache filled my heart. Once probate concluded, Tater would be officially mine. I already loved him—more than I'd imagined I could in such a short time. If the inn went out of business, his life would change too. Would he be happy at my house back in Kansas City?

I ran a hand along his back. He had such thick, luxurious fur that he reminded me of a stuffed animal.

"Only you're much better than a stuffed animal, aren't you, Tater?" I'd known shy cats, aloof cats, and mellow cats. I'd never known a cat that was so affectionate.

He looked up and blinked.

"You know, Tater, I am really good at talking to people. Or, more importantly in this situation, at getting people to talk to me." One of the developers back at the office in

Kansas City had told me that with the exception of her therapist, I was the best listener she'd ever known.

Tater kneaded my leg.

I continued petting him, my stress melting away. "I know I'm not a real detective, but would it hurt to ask a few questions? To sit around with Kate and Addison and think about the murder logically?"

Tater purred in encouragement.

"They both have all sorts of local connections. If we need info, we could probably get it."

Tater rubbed his cheek against my tummy.

"It would be helping the inn. Even if we implement all the best ideas in the world, we can't be a success with a murder casting a shadow over the place."

Tater adjusted his position. If I kept sitting here, he might take a nap right on my lap.

I lifted him into my arms, held him like a baby, and rubbed under his chin. "Thank you, Tater. You've helped me calm down enough to see the best path forward. Even if I feel a little nervous about this, I can't sit by and let Kate's sister be blamed for J.B.'s death. And if I want the inn to be a success, I can't let this situation go on longer than it has to."

The front door opened, and Addison appeared. "I'm back. Grandpa and I got things mixed up. The meeting is tomorrow, and I thought of one more improvement I can make to the reservation system."

"I'm glad you're here." I set Tater back on the floor. "Can

you come with me? I need to talk to Kate, and I want you there as well."

Addison's eyes narrowed. "You're not giving up on the inn already, are you?"

I shook my head and led the way to the kitchen, where Kate had the AC set to maximum cool. She stood at the stainless-steel island slicing fresh pineapple.

"I've been thinking about your sister, Kate." I stepped closer.

She laid down her knife and wiped her hands on a nearby towel.

"If Cal Granger isn't going to look for other suspects in J.B.'s murder, I want to. Would you and Addison be willing to help me?"

Addison gasped, and Kate's eyes welled with tears.

"Yes—yes—a thousand times, yes!" Kate cried. "Thank you!"

"I'm on board," Addison said, nodding. "Whatever you need."

"I think we should give this a shot," I said. "It may not work, but we might find the real killer and prove that Kate's sister is innocent."

"I know we can," Addison said. "Look at what we figured out when you came for that visit in April."

Kate pulled us both into a tight hug.

My heart swelled.

Addison's phone, then mine, dinged in quick succession. Her face lit, and she pulled her phone from her back pocket. "I think that's the ringtone I set for the— It is! We just got our first online booking!"

The three of us cheered, and Addison proudly showed us how the app displayed the new information.

We were a team—a team that could make improvements to the inn and, with luck, figure out who committed the murder.

Chapter Six

"You'll love the path around the lake," I said the next morning to the couple staying in the suite. "Feel free to grab a water bottle from the little fridge by the door."

The woman's eyes lit. "Oh, thank you. I meant to bring our reusable ones, but I forgot."

"Happy to help," I replied. "Have fun."

Tater, who was sitting on the end of the check-in desk, looked over at them expectantly.

The woman told him good morning and rubbed his ears. The man bent to tie the laces on one of his tennis shoes, then the two of them headed out to the patio.

I sat back down behind the desk and congratulated myself. In spite of the murder, these guests seemed happy. Little by little, I was getting better at handling all the issues involved in running the inn.

Hopefully, Kate, Addison, and I could also make progress in finding J.B.'s killer.

According to Kate, Lena had been held at the police station for six hours yesterday but had eventually been released. We'd made plans to talk to her after lunch. She knew J.B. better than most, and she'd been at the police station where she might have heard officers talking. With luck, she'd have some information that could help us.

An hour later, Kate texted to say she'd finished everything she needed to do in the kitchen, then she rushed into the lobby. "Let's go see Lena."

I made sure the sign with my cell phone number was on the desk and grabbed my purse.

Kate drove us to the library in her red Mustang convertible. She kept the top up, the AC blasting, and as she drove, gave me a guided tour of Claremont, pointing out all the locally owned restaurants and shops.

Once the murder was solved, I'd have to make time to explore. Who wouldn't want to visit a shop that sold handmade chocolates or one that made luxury soaps and lotions? Or eat ice cream sitting under those umbrellas on the waterfront? It was all so pretty, with wooden barrels of flowers outside every shop door.

Kate gestured past the tourist shopping area toward the public beach, a lakeside park, and upscale lakefront apartments and homes. Claremont, she said, boasted some of the best restaurants in a four-county area, had a rich history of supporting the arts, and had won an award for being one of the most bike-friendly small towns in the state.

At a light, she turned and headed away from the water.

Soon, we pulled up in front of the Claremont Public

Library, which featured a large array of solar panels on the roof. As we headed up the walk, we passed a flower bed labeled "Project Pollinator." Bees drifted from flower to flower, and a monarch butterfly rested on a dwarf butterfly bush, enjoying its vivid purple blossoms.

Inside, the distinct "library feel" washed over me—the soothing quiet, the reassuring smell of paper and ink, and the comfort of being surrounded by people who loved books. Had I ever walked into a library and not felt happy?

Nope.

Beyond an art exhibit by local high school students, Lena gave a shy wave from the central checkout desk.

Kate and I headed toward her, but a little girl of about four raced past us, cutting us off.

"Miss Lena!" she cried. She ducked under the fold-down counter that closed the circle of the desk and hugged Lena's legs.

The girl's mother hurried over, pushing a stroller holding a baby gnawing on a teething biscuit. "Cassidy," she said with a note of exasperation in her voice. "You're not supposed to go inside the circle of the desk, remember?"

Interesting. The news that the librarian had been questioned by the police had to be all over town, but Cassidy's mom's body language didn't communicate any worry about her child's safety with Lena, merely a desire for the child to follow the rules. In fact, I got the distinct impression that, given the chance, the mom would have happily left both her kids with Lena for the rest of the day.

One more reason to believe that Lena wasn't a killer.

Eventually, after Lena told the mom about a new book Cassidy would love, the family made their way to the children's section, and Lena called over a co-worker to cover the desk. Then she led Kate and me to her office in one of the wings of the building.

Her office suited her: pale blue binders neatly arranged on the shelves, a soft watercolor of cherry blossoms on the wall, and a miniature fountain gurgling atop the shelves.

"I'm surprised you came in to work today," I said after she closed the door and we sat down. "Kate told me Cal Granger kept you at the police station until late last night. I'd think you'd be exhausted."

"I am." Lena ran a fingertip under one eye. "If it wasn't for this undereye concealer, you'd see the dark circles, but I couldn't sit at home. I'd worry myself sick. At least here, I have other things to think about." She pulled her chunky indigo cardigan closer around her shoulders. "Sorry about the chill in here. The AC seems to be working overtime ... or maybe I'm simply exhausted."

"Tell us about J.B.," Kate said. "Who do you think killed him?"

Lena answered in her soft, gentle voice. "I will, but first I want to thank you, Meredith." She gave me a heartfelt glance. "You've only known Kate a short time and barely met me. I really appreciate that you're willing to believe I might be innocent."

"Why don't you tell us the whole story?" I asked.

"Gladly." Lena scooted a small vase of wildflowers farther to the side of her desk and leaned forward. "I started seeing J.B. six months ago. I know he rubbed a lot of people the wrong way, but he had a softer side. And he didn't always give that impression, but he was quite well read. That's important to a librarian." She offered a sad smile. "I'll admit, I was beginning to think maybe this relationship might be long term." Lena looked over at me. "I was married before, but we only had a year before my husband died in a boating accident. Since then ... well, it took a lot for me to think about a permanent commitment."

"I'm so sorry." How awful for Lena. At least I'd had more than two decades with my Clint. Being widowed fairly young myself, I understood how that loss could affect your view of relationships.

None of this explained why she was considered a suspect. "So, what happened next?"

Lena's jaw tensed, and she pulled her auburn hair forward over one shoulder. "About two weeks ago, I learned J.B. had completely deceived me. Almost the entire time we'd been together, when I'd thought we were in an exclusive relationship that might lead to marriage, he'd been seeing someone else."

My chest tightened. How horrible.

Kate's jaw tightened. "I know you told me at the time, but it still makes me furious."

"It made me furious too. I figured it out one night when we were at Kelsey's Bar and Grill. It's a townie place," she added, glancing at me, "out of the way so most tourists don't find it."

I'd never heard of it, but I waited for her to continue.

She brushed at a miniscule crumb on her desk.

"And?" I asked.

She blinked and looked a bit like she might throw up, then blurted out the rest. "When, like an idiot, I finally put it all together, I just lost it. It had been so hard for me to trust in a relationship and to learn it was all a lie... I'd ordered chicken-fried steak and mashed potatoes, and Kelsey's has these huge steak knives. Before I even realized what I was doing, I picked up the knife and told J.B. to get out of my sight before I stabbed him right in his lying, cheating heart."

"Lena!" Kate's mouth dropped open. "You didn't tell me that."

Lena winced. "Well, I'm not proud of it. I didn't say it very loudly, but someone in the next booth must have overheard me and told Cal Granger every word." She blew out a long breath. "But it was nothing but talk. I wouldn't have really done it. J.B. kept justifying what he'd done and trying to make me feel like I was overreacting, and I wanted him to shut up and leave."

Whew. I ran a hand over my mouth. All that, plus she'd been the first person at the scene of the murder. No wonder Cal Granger had zeroed in on her. I looked over at Kate.

"I don't care," Kate said firmly. "I know you, Lena. You're quiet, quiet, quiet, and then *boom*—you explode. But you'd never hurt anyone, and after you get mad, you don't stay mad for long. You're not comfortable with anger. Besides, this happened, what, two weeks ago? By the time of the reception, you were probably telling yourself that this was a blessing in disguise, that at least you'd learned J.B.'s true measure before you married him."

Lena shifted her weight in her chair and raised one eyebrow. "Miss Amateur Psychologist, huh?" She shrugged. "You're not wrong. I did feel like I'd started to move past it. Unfortunately, Cal doesn't see it that way."

I looked from Lena to Kate and then back again. I'd always felt I had a good inner sense of when people were telling the truth. Both what Lena said and how Kate had explained her sister's personality made sense. Oh, I couldn't say I believed Lena 100 percent. There was still a hint of doubt in my mind. J.B.'s betrayal had been heartless, particularly as he must have known how hard it was for Lena to love again after losing her husband. I couldn't imagine how painful that must have been.

But I certainly thought we should look at other possible suspects. "You knew a lot about J.B.'s life, Lena. Is there anyone you think might have had a reason to kill him?"

Lena nodded emphatically. "Tony."

"Tony Rossini, the guy who got him out of the water?" I asked.

"It was his wife that J.B. was seeing," Lena said.

Kate slapped both hands on the desk. "I had no idea."

"Neither did Tony, apparently," Lena said. "After I got so mad at J.B. at the bar that night, I heard that eventually somebody told him. And Tony's got a real temper. We went through school together, so I know."

"By wading into the hot tub to get J.B. out and doing

CPR, he had a reason for his DNA to be on J.B.'s body," I said slowly.

"So why isn't Cal investigating him?" Kate asked.

"I tried to tell Cal about Tony," Lena said. "He acted like I was just trying to pin the blame on someone else. I don't even know if he's questioned Tony."

"Well, someone should." I glanced over at Kate.

Maybe Cal didn't have as much of an instinct about people as I did, didn't have the same gut feeling that Lena was innocent. "If I have a casual chat with Tony, he might let slip some clue I can pass on to Cal, something that will open his eyes and make him see Tony as a real suspect."

"Thank heaven." Kate stood. "At least somebody in this town has some sense."

Chapter Seven

By two o'clock, Kate and I were nearly back to the inn. Off to the southwest, clouds churned, the sky grew darker, and thunder rumbled.

Kate, though, seemed unconcerned about the approaching storm. "I can't thank you enough, Meredith, for listening to Lena and keeping an open mind."

"Well, her admission that she threatened to stab J.B. was pretty disconcerting," I admitted.

"It sure surprised me, but I know it was just talk," Kate said. "After hearing about Tony, I think he has to be the killer."

"I'm still keeping an open mind," I said. "I'm not coming to any conclusions until I learn more."

Kate shook her head as if I was missing the obvious. A few minutes later, she parked at the side of the inn, and we raced for the kitchen door, barely making it in before thunder cracked and rain began to pour down.

"Just in time," she said. "And just in time for me to get the appetizers ready for teatime." She hurried toward the kitchen.

I walked into the lobby and saw Addison, who was headed out to pick up her grandfather to take him to his service club meeting.

"Try to stay dry," I called after her.

"Yeah, right." She pulled up the hood on her rain jacket, and her light laughter floated back to me.

I wandered to the windows that looked out over the lake. The rain came down in sheets. Tree branches jerked in the wind. Even from up here on the hill, I could see whitecaps on the water. Quite a storm, but cocooned inside the inn, I rather enjoyed the show.

Eventually, I took the chair behind the desk and began ordering the new bedding.

Even if I decided not to keep the inn after probate concluded, these were solid investments in the business. There was no reason to delay the purchases any longer.

By six that night, when we closed the desk, two more guests had checked in.

I rather prided myself on how quickly I was learning the guests' names. Eric and Rachel were the athletic-looking thirty-something couple who had been here last night and hiked around the lake earlier, when the weather was so nice. Neil, who had just checked in, was a heavyset traveling sales rep who seemed rather stressed. He'd told me how much he valued the quiet of the inn when his route took him through our part of the state. Mavis, the other newcomer, was a slender woman in her early eighties on her way home from visiting an old college roommate.

Mavis had booked the ADA room, but when she checked in, she proudly told me she didn't really need it anymore. She'd made the reservation shortly after she'd had surgery. Physical therapy, she claimed, had worked miracles. She happily declined my offer of help with her luggage and rolled her suitcase toward her first-floor room.

Two hours later, after I'd eaten some dinner in my quarters, I wandered through the first floor. The sky was dark as another wave of the storm passed through, so I flipped on lights and made sure the little sign that said "Our Front Desk is Closed for the Night" was readily visible with my cell number in case of emergency. All was as it should be, snug and cozy and ready for the night.

I glanced over at Tater, who had settled himself on the end of the reception desk and curled up in a ball. "Want to come with me, big fella? I think I'll make myself some popcorn and—"

Lightning struck very close, thunder boomed, and the lights went out.

I heard Tater leap to the floor and scamper away, and I raised a shaking hand to my heart. The entire inn had been plunged into darkness. The cozy feeling was gone, replaced by pitch black creepiness.

"Meredith? I was still here doing some breakfast prep. You okay?" Kate approached, holding one of the tea-light candles from a table in the dining room.

"I'm fine. Just startled. We don't, by chance, have a generator, do we?"

"No such luck," Kate replied.

"You mean we're stuck here in the dark until the power company gets around to repairs?" Neil's voice had a distinct whine as he made his way down the stairs using his phone for light. "What a nightmare. The place was just the scene of a murder and now there's no power."

"I'll go call the utility service." Kate pulled out her phone and stepped away.

"Thanks." That left me to deal with one—uh, four—whiny guests. Rachel, Eric, and Mavis all had joined Neil in the lobby, and none of them seemed particularly pleased. Or understanding.

I rushed to offer my apologies. "Hopefully, the power will be back on in a few minutes."

"I sort of doubt it," Kate said under her breath as she walked back beside me. "This whole part of town is out of power and so is the area over by the school complex."

Eric apparently overheard what she said and told the others. The news didn't make anyone any happier.

Okay, I told myself, this was not a true emergency. Everyone was safe and dry. Even if the power didn't come back immediately, as long as none of the food spoiled in the kitchen, it was simply an inconvenience. I pressed my lips together. How could I reframe the situation?

"Kate," I whispered, "does the fireplace work in the parlor?" I knew it held neatly stacked wood, but that might only be for show.

"It works," she said. "We use it in the winter, just like the matching one in the lobby across the hall. In the summer, though, we use the fire pit because it's so nice outside." She gave the windows overlooking the lake a withering glance. "Well, normally it's so nice." Rain was coming down in torrents.

"You don't have marshmallows, do you?" I asked. "We could probably cheer everyone up if we roasted some over the fireplace."

Her eyes lit. "Most of the time I'd say no, but I bought some recently for a special brownie recipe. We even have roasting sticks that we sometimes use at the fire pit." She looked up and off to one side, as if remembering where they were stored. "I'll do you one better," she said. "How about s'mores made with thin chocolate wafer cookies and Andes mints?"

I could have hugged her. "Gourmet dessert. You are a genius!"

I beckoned the guests closer. "I have to tell you all, I have two favorite kinds of dessert."

Their facial expressions ranged the gamut from exasperation to confusion.

"Hot," I deadpanned. "And cold."

Mavis's lips twitched and Rachel snickered.

I was no comedian, but it might have warmed them up a little. I shared our s'mores plan, said it counted as a "hot" dessert, and suggested we could play a board game. Games always made me happy. Maybe it would cheer them up as well.

Three of the guests good-naturedly got on board. Neil, though, stood with his mouth twisted up. He scowled at the stairs and then with obvious reluctance admitted that he did love s'mores.

Using our phones for light, we split up to get ready. Rachel and Eric headed back to the kitchen with Kate to get the supplies for the s'mores as well as more candles. Mavis found the board games in a bookcase in the library and suggested that Neil help her pick one out. And I went to the storage closet on the second floor, where Kate told me I should find the roasting sticks.

When I returned, a toasty fire burned in the fireplace, and the group had brightened the room with candles and spread out the food. Rachel was already sampling the chocolate mints. Kate had opened an antique game table we normally kept folded against the wall, Eric was drawing up chairs, and Neil was setting up Scrabble.

"It's designed for a maximum of four, but we can play in teams," Mavis said.

Before long, we had each eaten at least two minty s'mores, and Kate had been lauded as an even greater culinary genius than before. After removing the goo from our fingers, we all joined in a game of Scrabble. Mavis and Neil formed a team, the married couple—Rachel and Eric— formed a second, and Kate, who normally left as soon as the kitchen was cleaned, called her neighbor to ask him to check on her dog, and stayed to be my partner.

"I can't resist a board game," Kate said. "Growing up

with two sisters, I played all the time. Not that I'm competitive or anything," she added with a grin.

"Ah, so you're saying you're an expert, huh?" Eric laughed. "Just wait until you see the words Rachel comes up with." He grinned at his wife.

Tater reappeared, nuzzled my ankles, and hopped up on the couch beside Mavis, who obligingly scratched his ears. As the game progressed, he watched the tiles being arranged on the board but resisted the urge to bat them around until one fell on the floor.

Then he pounced on it and flicked it under the couch.

Rachel got down on her hands and knees and retrieved it. "Sorry, buddy, we need this one. It's a precious commodity, a blank tile." She gave him a pat on the head and returned the tile to the bag.

"Thanks for getting that," I said.

"No worries." She grinned. "We have a cat at home. My sister's watching him."

Deprived of his prize, Tater hopped back up by Mavis as if he'd decided it was his official place in the group.

As a swirl of happiness filled my chest, I realized we had indeed bonded into a group. For me, the guests weren't just names I was trying to remember, and for the guests, the board game wasn't just a way to pass the time. They were laughing and smiling and truly enjoying themselves. My plan had worked out even better than I could have hoped. What could have been a disaster of an evening had become, Mavis said, a highlight of her visit.

The tiles dwindled down until Rachel played the last one.

Eric, who'd volunteered to keep score, did some final calculations and right as he declared Mavis—who had turned out to be the best player by far—and Neil the winners, the power came back on.

The guests cheered, but no one rushed upstairs. And Neil, the same guy who'd been reluctant to join in the fun, suggested another round.

Kate bowed out, saying she needed to get home. With all four of our guests checking out the next morning, I did as well, knowing I'd need plenty of energy to help Addison clean rooms.

So, I left the four of them, supervised by Tater, enjoying their game by the fire. For the first time since the murder, the inn didn't feel shadowed by loss. It felt full of warmth and promise.

Chapter Eight

WHEN I SAID goodbye to our four guests the next morning, I found myself hoping that each of them—even Neil, who had at first seemed a bit of a pill—would come back soon.

Then I helped Addison turn over the rooms. To my surprise, she was excited to hear of our impromptu game night and made me promise to text her if we ever held another one. As we worked, I learned that, unlike what I'd suspected, she didn't start on the same floor each time she cleaned or even do the tasks in each room in the same order.

"Too boring," she said. "I have to mix it up."

Fascinating. She'd taken a very routine job and found a way to make it fit her personality. I followed her lead and did the tasks she suggested.

After the inn was in order, I made sure Tater had fresh food and water and cleaned his litter boxes. Once that was taken care of, with no reservations for the night, I decided that if I was going to figure out who killed J.B., I needed to get more information.

I hopped in my SUV and headed over to Bellamy Lake—about a forty-minute drive, even though it was only twenty miles as a crow flies. I pulled into a parking spot in the large lot at Bellamy Pointe, the upscale hotel run by Tony Rossini.

Seven stories tall, Bellamy Pointe featured bold modern architecture and striking landscaping. Inside, the two-story lobby gleamed, and a fountain in a modern, asymmetrical style gurgled softly. It offered bellmen, valet parking, and room service.

A desk clerk, who wore a pale cream suit and who could have doubled as a runway model, welcomed me. The contrast between her and me, greeting guests in denim capri pants and one of my better flowered T-shirts, couldn't have been more distinct.

The Roseview Inn—and its new owner—seemed like the dowdy stepsister.

My mind started down a dreary path of comparisonitis until I noticed a piece of art in the lobby. I was almost certain I'd seen that exact same print in my dermatologist's office back in Kansas City.

Maybe that was something the Roseview Inn offered: individuality.

After all, one high-end hotel might seem a lot like the next.

And—I thought back to last night—the Roseview Inn was homier and more restful. Not everyone wanted a hotel with a nightclub in the lobby and a view of a lake filled with speedboats.

Plus, there was something about an inn built in 1902 and furniture handmade with time and care that put things in perspective. The Roseview Inn and the objects inside it had been with people when they'd faced hardships and been with them when they'd overcome them. The long existence of the inn and its antiques silently spoke, in a way, of resilience. That in itself was comforting.

I squared my shoulders and approached the desk.

A minute later, Tony came from around a corner. "Meredith! What a nice surprise! Come, let's talk in my office."

Tony's office was decorated in the same upscale fashion as the lobby, with a huge, gleaming wooden desk, sleekly upholstered chairs, a giant art print on one wall, and several local business awards on another.

An award … could the Roseview Inn win one someday?

I drew my attention back to Tony. "I didn't get a chance to speak with you properly at the reception," I began.

We shared an uncomfortable moment as we both remembered the tragedy.

"So unfortunate." Tony smoothed his dark beard.

"I wanted to let you know how much we appreciate it when you send your overflow guests to the Roseview Inn. I'm sure in time we'll build more clientele seeking the slower pace of Lake Claremont, but in the meantime, we're glad for the referrals."

"Happy to send them your way," Tony said. "Both of

these lakes offer such natural beauty. The more time tourists spend here, the more they will want to come back. Each time either one of us ensures a tourist has a great stay, we help guarantee there's plenty of business to go around."

Well, that was a refreshing attitude, much more encouraging than I'd expected. I'd planned this part of the conversation as a subterfuge to get to a point where I could question him about the murder, but I was actually building a professional relationship.

"Just so you know," I added, "we're planning some upgrades, starting with king beds."

"Good call. Those smaller beds have limited the referrals we could send your way at times. I can even tell you where we get our mattresses. I've found a local place I really like." He gave me a name and the saleswoman he dealt with.

"Thank you," I said sincerely. "Both for your encouragement and your generous attitude."

He sat back in his chair, the picture of a man so successful that he could afford to help the little guy—or gal, in this case.

Now, though, things might get sticky. I needed to steer the conversation around to questions about the murder. I drew in a deep breath and plunged in.

"I also wanted to thank you for springing into action with CPR the other day. It didn't end as we'd hoped, but I really appreciate your skills and your willingness to help."

He brushed my comment aside with one deeply tanned hand. "I'm sorry Vanessa and I couldn't save him."

"Such an unfortunate event," I said. "I don't know why

—maybe because I'm new to the area—but people keep telling me things about J.B. Things that seem to indicate that a lot of people had reason to hate him, even you."

A half second passed, and then Tony narrowed his eyes at me. "Weaving some sleuthing in with hotel management, Meredith?" He gave a wry laugh. "I'm guessing someone told you about my wife's affair with him."

My chest tightened. I thought I'd been subtle. Apparently not.

"No need to beat around the bush," he said. "I'll tell you flat out, I didn't kill J.B."

I kept silent, partly out of nervousness and partly because I hoped he'd say more.

"My wife's affair with J.B. was, unfortunately, not an isolated incident. If it hadn't been him, it would have been some guest here at the inn. So, while I am angry about what went on, I'm enough of a realist to recognize that J.B. wasn't the problem." Tony rested his elbows on the arms of his desk chair and steepled his fingers. "It's time for me to talk to a good divorce lawyer."

"I'm so sorry."

He let out a heavy sigh. "I imagine Kate got you involved in this, and I sympathize. I think Cal Granger's off on the wrong track, suspecting Lena."

"Oh?" I scooted forward in my chair. "Do you suspect someone else?"

He leaned back and studied me. Eventually, he sat up straight. "If I were Cal, I'd be looking at Elliot."

"Elliot Renner, the art gallery owner?" The thin man had seemed too nervous to kill someone.

"I know, I know." Tony grinned. "He looks about as threatening as a chipmunk. But a week before the murder, J.B., Elliot, and I sat out on the back deck of J.B.'s restaurant playing poker while the staff was cleaning up inside. I left to take a call in private and when I came back, Elliot took a swing at J.B."

"Really?"

"Really. They'd both had too much to drink, especially J.B., or I think he would have pummeled Elliot. I told them both to sleep it off and drove Elliot home."

Tony's jaw tightened. "The next day, someone broke the news to me that J.B. had been seeing my wife. That was the Friday of Memorial Day weekend. The hotel was a madhouse, which was stressful enough, and I felt like a chump for playing poker with J.B. the previous night. He probably thought it was hilarious that I sat there, not know-ing." The tendons in his neck grew rigid. "At least I didn't lose any money to the guy."

I shifted in my chair. If I'd been Tony, I'd have been furious.

"Anyway, I know J.B. had been drinking a lot at your reception. If Elliot was still angry about whatever upset him when we were playing cards, he might have seen it as a good time to take J.B. unawares."

"Gosh." This entire conversation had gone differently than I'd expected.

Tony stood. "Anyway, Meredith, I'm no murderer. And

I'm genuinely excited for the Roseview Inn with you at the helm."

"Thank you. I look forward to seeing you around." I got to my feet. "Are there local Chamber of Commerce meetings?"

"There are. Boring as all get-out, but we both need to be there." He laughed and walked me to the lobby.

I drove back to the inn, wondering how I could manage the next conversation in my investigation more smoothly. Because I definitely wanted to talk to Elliot.

Without him realizing I thought he might be the killer.

I sat at the desk during check-in time, from three until six that evening, on the off chance that someone would walk in and want a room.

No one did.

With no one to serve afternoon tea to, Kate finished up early.

By seven, I'd eaten dinner, and she was gone.

The inn was empty except for me and Tater, who was curled up in a cushy chair in the library, asleep. I left a note on the door with my number, walked past, and refrained from giving Tater a pat so that I wouldn't disturb his slumber. Then I slipped out the back door and followed the path down to the lake.

Once beside the lake, I headed east, away from Claremont, enjoying the hum of insects, the reflection of the sunset on the water, and the lap of waves against the shore. I could get spoiled, living with all this beauty right outside.

I soon heard the jingle of dog tags, and Marshall appeared from around a bend, leading his human along behind on a leash.

"Meredith!" Philip gave me a wide smile.

"Nice to see you."

Marshall trotted over to me, and I told him hello and gave him a pat.

"I've been hoping I might run into you," Philip said. "I learned the most fascinating thing about the inn the other day."

"You did?" How perfect. The Roseview Inn would be even more attractive to guests if I had great stories to tell about it and the man who built it.

"Did you know that there's supposed to be something valuable hidden on the property?"

My heart jumped, but common sense quickly kicked in. "You're joking, right?"

"I'm not. I've been reading an old diary I found behind some other books on a high shelf at the library. Do you know much about the man who built Roseview?"

"No, I hardly know any of the details of the history of the place. If that history includes directions to a buried treasure, I'm more than ready to listen."

Philip beckoned me to a couple of chunks of limestone at the side of the path. "Sit down and let me tell you."

I eagerly followed him and sat on one of the rocks.

"Marshall, lie down," Philip said.

The German shepherd lay down in the grass between us and let out a contented snuffle.

Philip patted him on the head. "Good boy."

"The Roseview Inn was originally a private home," Philip began. "It was built by Horace Reed. He's one of the mine owners who will be the focus of my book."

I nodded. I remembered that Philip was a history professor here on sabbatical to write.

"About thirty years later, in the 1930s after the mines were depleted, the Claremont River was dammed to create hydroelectric power, forming Lake Claremont. The mines were covered by water, and Roseview became lakefront property."

"I guess it was too high to be flooded and in just the right spot," I said.

He nodded. "It was. And over time, Claremont transitioned from a mining company town to a tourist town."

"So was Horace the one who hid this valuable item on the property?"

"No," Philip replied. "He sold off the mines, became convinced his former workers were out to kill him, and died a few years later. The house passed to his younger brother, Jasper. He's the one credited with planting the original rosebushes and naming the place Roseview. And, in a fascinating turn of events, he was accused of murder. He mysteriously disappeared in 1905."

"No way." I couldn't believe Kate and Addison hadn't told me this. "Do you know what happened to him?"

"I don't think anyone does," Philip said. "But the diary I

read, which was written by his housekeeper's daughter, claimed that before he disappeared, he hid something valuable on the property."

"Does it say what it was?"

"No. Only that it was 'hidden by a rose.'"

My shoulders fell. "There have to be more than thirty rosebushes on the property." Even worse, I had no way of knowing if any of them had been alive in Jasper's time or if they had been moved. "Still, the idea of a buried treasure is pretty intriguing."

Philip's eyes lit. "That's what I thought. If I were to find more clues in my research, maybe we could..." He hesitated as if afraid he'd overstepped.

For a few seconds I stared at him. Did I trust this man? Did I want him involved in finding what legally might be my treasure?

Well, I'd never have known about it if he hadn't told me. If he was trying to steal from me, he could have snuck around, searching the property after I went to bed. Most importantly, my gut said he was more interested in the historical meaning of the treasure than the monetary value.

"Would you like to work together to try to find whatever Jasper hid?" I asked.

"I'd love it." Philip's eyes shone. "I'll keep reading to see if I can find any more clues." He stood, and Marshall lurched to his feet. "I guess I'd better finish Marshall's walk before it gets dark."

"I should get back to the inn." I dusted off the back of my capri pants. "Keep me posted, okay?"

"Will do." He gave a quick wave and turned down the path away from me.

I headed back to the inn. I thought about texting Kate and Addison to ask about the treasure, but they'd both put in so many extra hours after Mrs. Everly died that I hesitated to intrude on their free time if it wasn't an emergency.

Instead, I called Tater into my apartment. In very un-catlike fashion, he actually came when I called. Once I topped off his food bowl, I looked Philip up online.

I thought he was who he said he was, but there was always a chance this "valuable item buried on the property" was some sort of scam. It wouldn't hurt to back up my intuition with a little research.

I made some popcorn, began nibbling, and searched the internet. After about two minutes, I found Philip's name and photo online. He was a full professor and seemed well-respected. Not a fly-by-night scammer. In fact, I had an expert historian researching the Roseview Inn.

I watched an old sitcom and drifted off to sleep, happily imagining myself digging up a chest of glittering gold that could fund every upgrade the inn could possibly need, including a generator for power outages.

Just think what it could mean if Philip and I found the treasure!

Chapter Nine

"ADDISON!" I hurried over as soon as I saw her the next day. "Did you know there's supposed to be something valuable somewhere on the property?" My words tumbled out.

"Hidden by a rose?" she said.

"Yes!" I nodded, but doubt grew in the back of my mind. If she knew about the hidden treasure, did that mean someone had already found it? Were my dreams of a chest of gold coins all foolishness?

She gave me a look of pity. "I'm sorry somebody told you about that. Tons of people have looked, but no one's ever found anything. It's nothing but an old wives' tale."

My heart sank. "No treasure?"

"No. The only thing that story has ever brought the inn is trouble. We even lost a rosebush because someone damaged the roots digging near it. All they dug up was a pile of those old-fashioned pull tabs from aluminum cans, the kind that used to come off the can, you know?"

I vaguely remembered seeing those when I was really young. Pull tabs were not the type of treasure I wanted to find. I let out a long sigh. "I guess we'll have to make money here at the inn the old-fashioned way."

"That's why I came in," Addison said. "All the equipment arrived to upgrade the Wi-Fi. I thought I'd get it set up before our new guests arrive tonight."

"Gosh, thank you. Do you need help?"

"No. I'm good." She smiled and headed back upstairs.

Probably for the best. With a little effort and sometimes an internet search for directions, I could use tech fairly well. Setting it up was—

I almost blamed my shortcomings on my age, but that wasn't right. Addison, like most of the people I'd worked with back in Kansas City, had a gift for computers and had taken classes to understand them better.

Age had nothing to do with it. My gifts were in other areas. No less important, just different.

She could set up the Wi-Fi, and—with the inn empty until the evening—I could get back to my search for J.B.'s killer.

It was time to talk to Elliot Renner.

Elliot's art gallery, the Wren's Nest, was on the southern end of the Claremont tourist area, a few minutes' drive from the inn. If there hadn't been a significant hill to climb on the way back, I'd have walked.

Once I stepped in the gallery, I realized that it wasn't that large but had been partitioned to allow Elliot to display a good deal of art. From around a wall, I heard him discussing a painting with a potential customer. I edged closer and took a look at the piece in question.

It was oversized, maybe forty by sixty inches, and to my untrained eye looked garish. Vivid orange and hot pink faces repeated across the canvas with slashes of thick black paint slicing into them. There was, I'm sure, deep meaning in the painting, but it wasn't meaning I understood. How could someone pay money to live with what felt almost like violence on their wall?

I backed away and rounded a corner. The deeper I walked into the gallery, the stronger the air conditioning seemed to blow. I rubbed my arms and kept looking.

More abstract art awaited me, including one piece that I could have sworn was hung upside-down. I continued wandering. Was there anything Elliot sold that I'd even understand?

I turned the corner and sucked in a deep breath.

This—this art spoke to me.

Before me on the wall were four small watercolors easily identifiable as Lake Claremont. One in particular caught my eye. It was titled "At Dusk," and had been painted in soft blues and purples with patches of golden light reflecting off the water. I could imagine it near the fireplace in the lobby, greeting guests as they checked in.

I moved closer to read the price tag in the lower left corner, and I felt a distinct pain in my chest. No way was that in the budget.

"Meredith, found something you like?" Elliot walked

toward me, hunched over slightly as if he'd never gotten comfortable with his height.

I'd been so absorbed by the painting that I hadn't realized the other customer had left.

"This is beautiful." I gestured to the painting I'd found. "In fact, all four of them are."

"You've got a great eye. Those are by an exceptionally talented young local artist. I can't make any guarantees, but I wouldn't be surprised if anything she creates turns out to be a very good investment."

Ooh, that made me want the painting even more. I gazed at it another moment. "It's way out of my price range, I'm afraid." And not why I'd come into the gallery. I needed to talk about J.B.'s death.

This time, though, I was going to be smart. No direct questions, simply a conversation to get the feel of the man. After all, he and J.B. were alone at the time their fight started. If Elliot lied to me, I had no way of proving it.

I turned to face him. "How are you doing after the other day at the reception?"

His thin face clouded. "It's just so shocking, thinking that someone killed J.B. when we were right there."

"I know," I said softly. "I barely met him, though. I hadn't quite made up my mind about what I thought of him."

"J.B. was … okay," Elliot said in a way that implied he hadn't liked him.

"Okay?" I asked. With a little encouragement, Elliot might open up.

He shifted his body weight from one foot to the other. "I recently played cards with him, and that evening pretty much summed up my experiences with him. I mean, I tried several times to give the guy a chance, but how much can you enjoy being around a man who tries to use two aces of spades in one deck?" The corners of Elliot's lips jerked down, and then he seemed to consciously force them up. "That action alone says he thinks you're stupid. We'd only bet twenty bucks, but ... well, I have a thing about dishonesty. It really, really bugs me."

So that's what the punch was about—or at least what seemed to be the case. "I get it. I believe in being honest too." I looked away. "I wonder if J.B. was dishonest in some other area of his life, and that's why he was killed?"

Elliot opened his mouth, closed it, and gestured to the painting I'd admired. "Would you like me to show you similar works that are less pricey?" he asked quickly. "Or could I offer you a cup of coffee? I just made a pot of my favorite hazelnut blend."

I was a tea drinker, so I declined the coffee, but I readily agreed to see more art. We walked farther back into the gallery.

He was nervous—that was obvious—and I sensed he was hiding something, but I wasn't going to directly question him.

In the back of the gallery, I heard what I thought was someone else working, but I wasn't sure. It could have simply been a fan rustling papers. I wasn't going to take a chance with questions that might upset him if the two of us were alone.

We rounded a corner, and Elliot showed me three larger watercolors, all less than half the price of "At Dusk."

None of them appealed to me in the same way, and I admitted as much.

"Kind of what I suspected," he said. "But it does bode well for those renovations you're planning for the inn."

I turned to him. How did he know about the renovations?

"Not used to the small town yet, I see." He chuckled. "If you so much as think an idea, it will probably be all over town by nightfall. What I meant was that if you've got such good taste in art, any renovations will probably turn out well."

"Thanks." He was right about adjusting to a small town. Life in Kansas City was not the same as life in a town like Claremont. "Maybe that rapid spread of information will make it easy for Detective Granger to solve J.B.'s murder."

Elliot raised an eyebrow at me. One of his overly large ears rose also. "Cal's a good guy, but he hasn't had much experience with murder investigations." He opened his mouth as if to say more, then closed it again as he had before.

I couldn't hold back my curiosity. "Is there someone you think might be responsible for killing J.B.?"

"No. No idea." He pinched his lips together. A second later, one word slipped out. "Vanessa."

"Vanessa? The real estate agent?"

He winced and nodded. "As we were walking into the inn, I overheard J.B. on the phone. He was saying terrible things about her reputation as a real estate agent, really discouraging whoever was on the other end of the line from working with her. And he didn't see it, but she was walking up from farther down in the parking lot. I'm sure she heard every word."

"Gosh. I had no idea."

"Real estate's cutthroat. Comments like that could really infuriate someone."

"Did you tell the detective?"

"I didn't." Elliot looked at the floor and scraped the side of one loafer against the tile. "I was so freaked out by the murder that I forgot. I guess I should go in and talk with him."

"That's a great idea," I said as I neared the door. "It would give Detective Granger someone to question other than Lena Quinn."

He murmured his agreement, but I got the feeling he might not go through with it. He had that same look my daughter used to have when she told me—phone in hand—that she'd get right on her homework.

However, there was nothing to prevent me from having a casual conversation with Vanessa. Afterward, if the theory still seemed valid, I could pass the information along to Cal.

Because it sure seemed as if Vanessa might have had a motive for murder.

Chapter Ten

ONCE OUTSIDE, I was immediately surrounded by a buttery, chocolatey aroma wafting out of the bakery next door, the Claremont Crust & Crumb. I wasn't actually hungry, so I steeled my resolve and walked to my car.

There, I checked the website for the furniture store Tony had recommended, plugged the address into my GPS, and headed out. An hour later, after meeting the saleswoman he suggested, I felt as if I'd made real progress on my goals for the inn. I'd been able to test several mattresses and found one that I liked and that the saleswoman assured me was widely popular with other people as well. Plus, she was more than willing to cut me a deal for a large order.

I headed back to the inn, eager to tell Addison and Kate that I'd found new mattresses and a possible new suspect—Vanessa. As I neared the bakery, though, my stomach growled. I couldn't really argue with timing like that.

I pulled into the parking lot behind the bakery. A

minute later I stepped inside. In the display case, neatly arranged rows of treats beckoned me, including some delicious looking brookies, one of my favorite desserts. Who could resist a treat with a brownie bottom and a chocolate chip cookie top?

I pointed toward them. "I'll take one of those and a cup of milk to go," I said to the young man behind the counter.

"Meredith, how great to run into you," came a voice from behind me.

I spun around and blinked. "Uh, hi." I'd been thinking of Vanessa a minute ago and here she was, blond hair, high heels, and all.

The young man handed me my milk and brookie and told me the total. I paid, and Vanessa asked for a half-dozen peanut butter cookies.

"I was hoping I'd see you around town," Vanessa said to me as she took the bag with her cookies and tapped her credit card to the machine. "I just heard that Elliot told you I was the person who killed J.B.—that he'd made me mad by bad-mouthing my business."

Holy cow. This town was even smaller than I'd imagined. And what I'd thought might have been a fan rustling papers must have definitely been someone else working in the gallery—someone who'd texted or called Vanessa.

However, if the opportunity to talk to a suspect was being given to me, I was going to take advantage of it. "Elliot did say that you had a good reason for being frustrated with J.B. I guess with the murder being a big topic of conversation, speculation is inevitable. It sounds like J.B. may have annoyed a lot of people."

"You can say that again." Her jaw tightened, just for a half-second, then she gave me a broad smile and led us away from the counter. "But when I met you, I got this feeling that the two of us could become good friends. So, I wanted to assure you—honestly, I didn't kill the guy."

"If he was criticizing your business, that does sound irritating though."

"It was, but he was only one person." She shrugged. "If someone is looking for a real estate agent, I'm sure they check online. I've got hundreds of good reviews. I mean, real estate is competitive, but not *life-or-death* competitive." She laughed. "Besides, I recently got a fantastic listing, Madge Pullman's house. That's going to bring in a major commission, and despite its high price, I think it will sell quickly. It's been so well-maintained."

She had to know I'd check her reputation online. If she was lying, it would be obvious. "I see your point. I do wonder, though, whether the police are looking at the right suspect. Lena Quinn doesn't come across as a killer to me."

"Is that what they're thinking? Because she learned he was seeing someone else and got mad at him?" Vanessa rolled her eyes. "Lena would never hurt anyone. She's one of the gentlest souls I know."

"That's how she struck me, but J.B. didn't just fall into that hot tub by himself," I said. "Someone killed him. As I'm sure you'll appreciate as a fellow businesswoman, I want this situation resolved quickly."

"It can't be good for the inn," she said slowly. "I'll do what I can to help. If I hear of anyone having family in and needing a place for them to stay, I'll suggest they come to you. I know you must want to make it more successful."

"Thank you." Maybe Elliot had been mistaken, and I'd judged her wrong. Her point about her reputation as a real estate agent did make sense, and I appreciated that she recognized how much the inn could mean to me.

She patted my arm and halfway turned toward the door. "I'll call you. We should do lunch one day." She gave a quick wave and dashed out the door with her bag of cookies.

I unwrapped my straw, took a long drink of my milk, and stopped at the trash can to dispose of the wrapper.

When I turned to leave, a young, plump, dark-haired woman stopped me, glanced at her phone, and tapped her chest. "Candace Wells. Claremont Realty. You must be Meredith, the new owner of the Roseview Inn."

"I am. Nice to meet you."

"I couldn't help but overhear," she said. "If you're trying to find the killer, I've got some information you need."

"Oh?"

"Vanessa would never speak badly of anyone, but if you're looking for someone who's likely to have killed J.B., there's common knowledge among the real estate community that you should hear."

I stepped back into an empty space near the door and gestured for her to continue.

Candace ran a hand through her curls. "I'm not saying

she did it or anything, but if you're asking who had motive, you should consider Shannon Lenox."

"The woman who owns the bookstore?"

"Now, I can't ever see her killing someone," Candace said, in an excited whisper. "But J.B. was really horrid to her."

"What did he do?"

"About six months ago, the lakefront property immediately north of his restaurant came up for sale. Shannon has been interested in moving to a place that's lakefront for quite a while. It would be better for the coffee shop part of her business if she had a nice deck looking out over the lake. It's a challenge to find the right property, though. There's only so much space between the marina and the park, you know what I mean?"

I pictured the shoreline in my head. "I haven't been to her shop yet, but it's on this side of the road, right?"

Candace angled her head. "Less than a block north of here. She's got money she inherited when her grandmother passed away. She could buy or even build lakefront, but it's a question of what's available in the location she wants. The tourist traffic likes that one little area."

"I understand," I said.

"So, when that empty lot came up for sale—I'll spare you the long story about the guy who owned it and wouldn't sell it for years—she was ecstatic and put in a bid. The next day, J.B. put in a higher bid and convinced the owner to take it right away, before she could offer more."

"That does sound rather unfair." For both Shannon and

the person selling the land. I would have thought they might benefit from a bidding war.

"To make matters worse," Candace continued, "J.B. put a parking lot on the land."

I blinked and thought about the downtown area. "Isn't there a large, free parking lot across the street from his restaurant?"

"Yep. Parking for his restaurant isn't an issue except if there's a festival or special event in town. It was selfishness, plain and simple. He didn't want Shannon to get that lot." Candace raised her eyebrows and shook her head, as if stunned that someone could be so mean.

Gosh. That made me feel almost sick to my stomach. "That's awful."

"That was J.B.," Candace said. "Vanessa put it really well once when we were talking. J.B. had a way of 'ruining things for people.'"

It sure seemed that way, and it seemed like he'd made a lot of enemies in town.

"Thanks for telling me all this," I said to Candace. "I appreciate getting your insight."

"No worries. I just thought you should know."

"Thank you."

She angled her head toward the counter. "Time for me to get some goodies to take back to the office. Oh, and we're the largest real estate agency in the area. Keep me in mind if you ever want to sell the inn." She slipped me her card.

I took it, walked out of the bakery, and headed toward my car.

I needed to visit the bookstore and have a conversation with Shannon. First, though, I wanted to talk to Kate and Addison.

When I got back to the inn, Addison had finished for the day, but both she and Kate were eager to discuss possible suspects. We arranged to meet at the staff fire pit at seven after Addison listened to a recorded lecture and took a quiz online, Kate drove her dog to the vet for a checkup, and I closed the desk for the evening and ate a quick supper.

In the meantime, since the three guests arriving had all indicated they would reach the inn at the end of check-in, around six, I decided to take advantage of the relatively cool day and get in a quick late afternoon walk along the lakeshore. If our plans for the inn were successful, I'd ordinarily be tied to the desk from three to six each afternoon. At this point, though, the chance of a guest arriving without a reservation was so low that I thought I could slip away.

Just in case, I left a note with my number on the front door of the inn.

I made my way down the steps to the lakeshore path, pondering the business owners who'd been on the patio at the time of J.B.'s death. From what I'd learned, J.B. wasn't the nicest man, but that didn't give anyone the right to kill him.

At the bottom of the hill, I turned east. After a few minutes, I reached the path to Philip's cottage. I continued on, passing a cluster of tiny white flowers, and eventually came to a secluded cove surrounded by cedar trees. I sat on a sawed-off tree stump and watched dragonflies dip over the water and bugs skim across the surface like ice skaters. About thirty feet out, a fish surfaced with a soft splash, and a circle rippled outward.

I inhaled deeply, exhaled, and let some of the tension in my shoulders melt away.

Certainly, the death of J.B. Hodges and its aftermath had been stressful. Mostly because I didn't believe Lena was the killer, so I wanted the real culprit brought to justice, but also because I didn't know who that was.

I got up, turned back, and continued my stroll, trying to focus more on the scenery than on murder.

"Meredith!"

I looked up the hill. I'd been so absorbed in my thoughts that I hadn't realized I was already back to Philip's cottage. "Oh, hello," I called.

"Just a moment," he replied. "I'll be right down."

There was a loud bark, and then, although I couldn't see him through the trees, Philip's footsteps echoed down the hillside along with the sound of Marshall's tags jingling.

"I'm glad I caught you," Philip said, appearing from around a curve in the path from his cottage. "I was on my porch and spotted you as you walked east. I was hoping I'd see you on the way back."

Marshall, too, was eager to see me, and started to jump up on me.

"Sit," Philip said firmly. "I'm sorry. I didn't take the time to grab his leash."

Marshall dropped to his haunches and gave us a look that said—except for the tiny issue of jumping on the unsuspecting—he was obviously the best dog in the whole state.

"Good boy," Philip said.

I patted Marshall's head and told him hello.

"How's your day been?" I asked Philip.

He laughed and looked down at Marshall. "Someone went for a swim in the lake this morning, then rolled in the dust and had to have a bath. So, I'd say my day has mostly been wet."

Marshall tipped his head and gazed at me. I swear, if he could talk, he would have told me Philip was lying.

"I was thinking about that offer to tour the inn," Philip said. "Is there a chance we might do that one day this week?"

"Of course! I'd love to show you the place. How about I check the reservations when I get back and get in touch with you then?"

His face lit. "Excellent. I'll be looking forward to it." He gave me his cell number.

We chatted a few more minutes about Marshall and the weather, and I made my excuses to head home.

"One more thing." Philip moved his hand as if he was going to touch my arm but didn't. "I heard about the murder. Have the police made any progress?"

"Not that I know of," I said. "The woman who's the chef

at the inn, Kate Brooks, is a wonderful person, and the police think her sister, Lena Quinn, is the murderer."

"Lena from the library?" Philip's brow furrowed.

I nodded.

"I've spent many hours at the Claremont Public Library. Lena does not strike me as a murderer."

"Me neither. That's why I've been, well"—I shifted my weight from one foot to the other—"doing a little investigating of my own."

He raised an eyebrow.

"People tell me things," I said. "I guess I'm easy to talk to. So, I thought if I had casual conversations with some of the people who also had opportunity to kill J.B., one of them might let something slip that I could pass along to the detective in charge. Maybe it would convince him to consider someone else as the killer instead of Lena."

"You are easy to talk to," Philip agreed. "But this could be dangerous. You might be setting yourself up to be the next target."

I bit my lip. I had been rather graceless when I talked to Tony. He'd seen right through me. "I was a little awkward at first," I admitted. "I've gotten better, sort of commiserating about what we all went through rather than pointing a finger or anything."

Philip didn't look as if he completely believed me, but he didn't say so. "That seems like it might be stressful."

"Not the conversations so much, but overall, yes, it is. I've talked with four of the five other people who were on the patio at the time of J.B.'s murder—other than Lena, me, and Addison, the desk clerk at the inn. I can't say for sure that any of them is a really good suspect. It's like everyone had a reason to be angry with J.B., but none of them seems upset enough to have killed him. I've got one more person to talk to, but I feel like I'm missing something."

"Would you—" We both spoke at once.

"Please." He gestured for me to go ahead.

I felt a bit silly, but I continued with the invitation I'd been about to extend. "Would you possibly be interested in coming over this evening a little before seven? I could give you a tour of the inn, and afterward you could join Kate, Addison, and me to talk about the different suspects. Maybe you'd see something we don't."

"I was about to ask if I could help in some way. So, yes, I'll be there."

"Oh, thank you." I gave Marshall another pat and headed home, my heart a little lighter.

Now I had an even bigger team, one that was more diverse. Philip could bring a whole different viewpoint to our discussions.

Surely, we could uncover J.B.'s killer.

Chapter Eleven

THE LAST FIFTEEN minutes of check-in were chaotic, with the three guests for the night, all singles, arriving one after another. The last one walked in the door a few minutes after six, but thanks to the new online system, I got him checked in quickly and smoothly.

Then I refilled Tater's bowl of kibble, texted Kate and Addison to let them know I'd invited Philip to join us, and ate a quick dinner. I had just run back downstairs when Philip walked in.

"Am I too early?" he asked.

"Not at all." I smoothed my shirt, hoping there weren't crumbs on it. "Let me show you the inn."

Tater sniffed at Philip's shoes and looked around. He then strode past, head high, as if to show one and all that he'd never been worried about a dog.

As Philip and I walked through the inn, I quickly learned that he saw the building in a completely different light than Kate, Addison, and me. Upgrades that we saw as exciting, such as the bathrooms that had been added to each guestroom upstairs in the 1980s, were ho-hum to him. The elaborate staircase, the large library, and the lobby—which, from what he'd read, must have once been Horace's office—were much more fascinating.

Eventually, after I promised to one day show him the carriage house, I led the way to the staff fire pit. Addison was already seated in one of the Adirondack chairs with her phone on her lap. The air was still quite warm, so a fire wasn't needed, and the four chairs were arranged so we could all enjoy the view.

I introduced Philip to Addison and, a minute later when she joined us, to Kate.

"You're Marshall's owner?" Kate asked.

"I am," Philip said. "I take full responsibility for whatever mischief he's gotten into."

Kate laughed. "He's a handsome dog. I'm sure he'll outgrow his puppy antics soon."

"From your lips to God's ears," Philip said, and he told us about the paper towel roll Marshall had knocked off the kitchen counter and had been unrolling to the other end of his cottage when he'd arrived back from the grocery store that afternoon. Luckily, Philip said, he'd arrived home before Marshall had eaten any paper towels.

We all chuckled.

"Ready to talk about the suspects?" I asked.

"That sounds so official." Addison grinned. "Like we're the Roseview Inn Detective Agency."

"Maybe the Roseview Inn Sleuths," Kate said. "Since we work for justice, not money."

I smiled. That actually had a nice ring to it.

Philip leaned in. "Before we discuss the suspects, can you tell me about the day of the murder? What exactly happened?"

Together, with each of us sometimes interrupting one another, Addison, Kate, and I talked him through the reception and the murder.

After a few minutes, Philip scratched the back of his head. "So, J.B. was hit with some blunt object, knocked out, and drowned. And he died in one of those built-in hot tubs that's below ground level, correct?"

The rest of us nodded.

"From what you've said, the hot tub and the fire pit are both hidden by the boxwoods?" Philip said.

"That's right," Kate said. "I don't think the police have found the weapon. At least, no one has taken our prints for elimination."

"Was the fire still burning after the police arrived?" Philip asked.

"It was," I said. Later that night, I'd poured water on it to make sure it was fully extinguished.

"The killer could have obtained a log from the woodpile, then used it to attack J.B. and push him underwater," Philip suggested. "Afterward, they could have tossed it in the fire. The murder weapon might now be nothing but ashes."

Addison's jaw went slack, and Kate and I exchanged glances.

"I never even considered that, but it makes perfect sense." It sure seemed like my decision to invite Philip had been a good one. "If that's what happened, though, it will make it even harder for Detective Granger to solve this crime." I let out a sigh.

"Which is why we're going to help him," Kate said. "Whether he wants it or not."

"I've been thinking about that," I said. "I wouldn't be surprised if people tell us more than they'd feel comfortable telling the police. So, Cal Granger's lack of progress may be understandable."

Kate gave a begrudging nod.

"I'm making notes on my phone," Addison said. "I'll send them to each of you with photos of the suspects I pull from online."

"That would be quite helpful." Philip gave her his number.

"Let's start with Tony Rossini," Addison said. "Owner of Bellamy Pointe, luxury hotel on Bellamy Lake." She turned to Kate and me. "Possible motive for killing J.B.?"

"J.B. was having an affair with his wife," Kate said. "While he was supposedly in a committed relationship with my sister Lena."

"But," I replied, "I didn't detect any real anger toward J.B. when I talked with Tony. He said if his wife hadn't cheated on him with J.B., she would have cheated on him with someone else."

Philip shifted in his chair. "I disagree." He rubbed his chin. "I went through a rather ugly divorce two years ago. I certainly take part of the blame for how things fell apart. I also blame my ex, who cheated on me for far too long without me realizing it." He shifted again, as if the chair had a splinter that was poking him. "But I never considered the guy she was seeing to be blameless."

Maybe I had been too trusting. Tony had been incredibly smooth. Maybe years of dealing with the public had taught him how to hide any anger. "I'm sorry about your marriage," I said softly to Philip.

"It's in the past." He rolled his shoulders back. "And I'm not saying I would have murdered the guy, but I was angry with him."

"Makes sense to me," Kate said. "No matter how charming Tony was when you talked with him, Meredith, he's still a suspect."

Addison typed into her phone and then looked up. "Elliot Renner, owner of The Wren's Nest art gallery. Motive?"

I leaned in. "He admitted he was mad that J.B. was cheating at cards even though they weren't playing for very high stakes."

"I guess, since Tony wasn't there at the time, we only have Elliot's word for what the bet was," Kate said.

"True," I admitted. "For all we know, they were playing for thousands of dollars."

"I've never gotten the impression Elliot had thousands of dollars to play with," Kate said. "I guess that might be the problem."

Addison made a note on her phone. "Okay, next we have Vanessa Moran, real estate agent."

"According to Elliot," I said, "J.B. bad-mouthed her business. She says she's got a great reputation and that one guy criticizing her wouldn't matter. I meant to look her up online. Is it true? That she's seen as a good agent?"

Addison pulled her phone from her back pocket, and her thumbs flew over the screen. "Yeah. Vanessa's got a lot of 5-star ratings."

Kate leaned back in her chair. "Playing devil's advocate here, but the fact that Vanessa's got that good reputation, which she worked really hard to get, might mean she resents anyone who tries to destroy it."

"Precisely," Philip said. "Any negative comments could cause her income to plummet."

"So, she's still a suspect." Addison typed more notes into her phone. "Next, Shannon Lenox."

Philip nodded. "I've met her,"

"I haven't talked with her yet," I said. "Though I did run into Candace Wells of Claremont Realty, and she seemed to think Shannon was a very likely suspect. Candace told me J.B. bought a piece of lakefront land out from under Shannon, one she really wanted so she could move her business to the side of the street by the lake. To make matters worse, he put an unnecessary parking lot on the land."

Philip scowled. "That's no way to treat a fellow member of your business community."

"Shannon stays on the suspect list," Addison said.

"So does Rita Alder," I added. "I don't know anything about her."

"She runs Claremont Gifts," Kate said. "I can't think of any tension I've heard of between her and J.B., but you never know."

"That means we haven't ruled anyone out," I said. "We started with five suspects, and we haven't made any progress."

"Not true." Addison set down her phone. "You've learned a lot, Meredith."

"Indeed," Philip said. "One thing I've found in my research is that you gather the pieces gradually. After you find the right piece, they all seem to fit together."

"Once we figure it out, I can take the information to Cal," Kate said. "I think if I approach him right, I can get him to accept our help without being defensive."

Hmmm. Given Kate's outspoken nature, the information might be better received coming from me, but I wasn't going to say that out loud.

Philip looked over at me. "You've done a great job, but you don't want to put yourself in danger. That talk you had alone with Tony, for instance, makes me uneasy. I can't help but think he's our killer. In the future, would you consider having these conversations in public locations?"

"I can do that." It was good advice.

"And if you're willing to take someone with you, I'm available," Philip offered.

"Me too," Kate and Addison chimed in.

"I want to talk to Shannon next," I said. "No direct questions, just to get a feel for her. I'll stop by her shop tomorrow afternoon."

"I can go with you," Kate said. "I want suspicion shifted away from Lena, but I don't want anything to happen to you." She reached over and squeezed my hand.

I looked at her and then at Addison and Philip. Gratitude welled up inside me. We were a good team. We'd figure this out.

Then Lena could go back to her normal life without the fear of arrest. Bookings at the inn could increase without the cloud of murder hampering our efforts. And I could continue with my plan to test out life in Claremont.

I couldn't wait to hear what Shannon had to say.

Chapter Twelve

The next afternoon, I was all set to go talk to Shannon when Addison stopped me.

"I was texting a friend of mine who goes to the bookstore every morning for coffee," Addison said. "He says Shannon takes off Mondays and Tuesdays and has her assistant cover the shop."

"Drat." I let my purse slide off my shoulder, and I tucked it under my arm. "Even if I learn where she lives, suddenly showing up at her house isn't going to seem very subtle, is it?"

Addison chuckled. "Kind of the opposite of subtle."

I blew out a long breath. I'd really been hoping to make progress today toward identifying J.B.'s killer. Unfortunately, it seemed sleuthing had a lot in common with running an inn—you had to be flexible.

"I guess it's a day for me to pay some attention to the

inn." I ran through my mental to-do list. "Before you head out, there's something I've been wondering."

"What?"

I pointed to the chandelier in the entry hall. Sunlight filtered in through the windows, illuminating dust motes that floated down onto the crystals and a cobweb that had appeared overnight. "How do you dust that thing? I've never noticed that you have wings."

Addison flapped her arms and laughed. "Once a year, we take it down and wash it. In between... C'mon. Let me show you the secret weapons for cleaning this place."

We went to the laundry room, and after Addison introduced me to cleaning tools that had never been needed in my ranch-style house back in Kansas City, I stood in the entry hall, watching her demonstrate how to use the duster with an extendable handle.

Tater sat on the landing of the main staircase below a geometric stained-glass window. He'd tucked himself between two spindles of the handrail and peered down, watching us.

When Addison stopped, I nudged her elbow and tipped my head toward Tater. "Someone's supervising you."

Addison chuckled. "Mrs. Everly was convinced that when he sat between those spindles, he thought he was completely invisible."

Invisible? Tater had to be close to fifteen pounds. He was in no way invisible between those narrow spindles. From the way he held his body, though, I could see why Mrs.

Everly had thought that. He did look like a cat hiding in the tall grass, ready to pounce.

"Got it," I said. "I'll pretend I don't see him."

"Aww, Meredith, you're good for the inn and good for Tater." She handed me the duster. "I'm so glad Mrs. Everly picked you and not that creepy third cousin." She gave me a sideways hug, said she had to run, and—while very obviously not looking toward Tater—headed through the dining room to go out the kitchen door.

Warmth filled my chest. What a sweet thing for her to say. She and Kate were good people.

Tater chose that moment to emerge from his hiding spot, come down the stairs, and nuzzle my leg. I scratched behind his ears, filled with gratitude for Addison's kindness and Tater's love.

After a moment, though, I looked back at the chandelier. I wanted to deal with that cobweb. I ran upstairs, got my earbuds, and lined up some '80s music to play through my phone.

With a bouncy dance tune playing for encouragement, I gripped the handle and raised the duster high. "Addison made this look easy, Tater."

It wasn't.

Despite the upbeat music, I quickly realized it took quite a bit of arm strength to control the duster and gently direct it without breaking any crystals on the chandelier.

Finally, when the cobweb was gone and my arm muscles began to ache, I collapsed the handle. "I think I'll give one of those special dusting cloths a try on the staircase instead of continuing to use this."

Tater followed me to the laundry room and back and then sat watching me, his head tilted to one side as if trying to discern what I was expending energy on. If it didn't involve trying to catch a bug outside, playing with a wadded-up piece of paper, or eating, Tater normally opted out and napped.

I studied the staircase. It went part way up to the second floor, turned at the landing with the stained-glass window, and continued. It had so much ornate carving that it really was a piece of art, but it also had a lot of crevices and edges to dust. Plus, since the area beneath the staircase wasn't open below the landing, there was a triangular side, crafted from the same beautiful walnut as the stairs, that blocked off the space underneath. I decided to start dusting there.

The triangular side had several panels, each edged with trim, like on a six-panel door.

I ran the cloth along the trim of one of the panels and rounded the corner to the trim on the underside edge of the panel. In contrast with all the other perfectly finished surfaces of the staircase, my cloth hit a bump.

That was odd. The staircase had clearly been made by a master craftsman. Maybe this section had been damaged and replaced at some point. I ran the cloth over the bump again and—

The whole triangular section on the side of the stairs popped out like a door on a hinge.

My chest tingled. I stared at the triangular door, which

was about five feet tall on one side and a foot tall on the other. I must have activated some spring mechanism, because it was now open about three inches on the short side.

I slid my hand into the opening and pulled the door toward me, revealing a storage spot under the stairs. There was a slight lip at the base so that when the door swung open, it didn't touch the floor. A musty, closed-up smell emanated from the space, and in the darkness I spotted what looked like a discarded wall sconce.

"I need a flashlight, don't I, Tater?"

The big cat poked his nose in, sniffed along the floor, and disappeared into the darkness.

"Wait for me!" I dashed behind the desk in the lobby and came back with the flashlight I'd stashed there after the power outage.

I shone it into the opening.

It looked as if no one had opened the door in decades. Cobwebs hung like straggly gray curtains from the underside of the stairs. Except for Tater's footprints, a thick layer of dust coated everything. The light fixture topped a pile of forgotten objects in the middle of the space. Underneath, I found an umbrella stand and an umbrella with a tortoise-shell handle, a mouse-chewed cardboard box, and an empty crate labeled "Apples".

I lifted the lid of the cardboard box and peeked inside. I found three carefully wrapped china cups with matching saucers.

"Holy cow, Tater, this is cool!" I looked around for him.

Tater had returned to the hall and was carefully cleaning the cobwebs from his whiskers.

Addison was gone for the day, but I ran to the kitchen and brought Kate back to see my discovery.

"I can't believe this was here all the time. I don't think Mrs. Everly knew about it. I'm sure Addison and I didn't," Kate said.

She peered in, then brought out one of the cup-and-saucer sets and flipped over the saucer. The pattern featured pink roses on a white background with gold accents. "It says Limoges."

"So, it's real porcelain, and that gold is probably real!" I said. Was this the treasure Philip had mentioned?

No, he'd said the valuable item was hidden by a rose, not decorated with roses. Besides, for a house this size, these cups seemed more like a normal purchase, perhaps to replace some china that had broken, not something considered out of the ordinary. Still... "They might be worth something!"

"Maybe not as much as you think," Kate said. "People aren't as excited by fine china as they used to be."

My chest deflated. She was right. I didn't think my adult daughter, Grace, or any of her friends would be excited to own the cups and saucers. "But they'd be fun to display."

"They would," Kate agreed. "It's so fabulous that you found them." We chatted another minute or two, but she soon said she had to get back to the kitchen to finish fixing an appetizer for teatime.

I sent Addison a quick text with photos, but she didn't

reply, and I wanted someone to continue to revel with me in my discovery.

Kate was cooking. Addison was clearly involved with something else. And Tater? I glanced over at him. He was fast asleep.

But I knew someone who lived close by who loved history. I quickly typed out a text to Philip.

Almost immediately, he replied.

PHILIP HOLT

I was just leaving the grocery store. Had to make an emergency trip because I ran out of coffee. Can I stop by and see your find?

Yes!

Five minutes later, after I'd brought the china out, carefully dusted it, and positioned it on the mantel in the parlor, I heard Philip come in the front door. I eagerly led him in to see the china and showed him the storage space.

"How exciting, Meredith!"

"Hold on." I leaned down in the storage space and pulled a fragment of a newspaper page from the floor. I carefully unfolded the top edge of the yellowed paper, afraid it might crumble. It was dated Oct. 5, 1905."

My heart sped up, and I held it so Philip could see.

"Would you look at that?" he said.

We both leaned in and began to read.

Deputy Sheriff Murdered

Deputy Sheriff Adam Chalmers was found dead in his home late Saturday evening.

Sheriff Hiram Barlow says Chalmers was a victim of foul play.

Chalmers, a longtime bachelor, lived alone. According to Nettie Haynes, who had worked for him for six years as a cook and housekeeper, Chalmers had invited four friends to join him for drinks and conversation Saturday at eight o'clock in the evening.

Saturday night, when the first two men arrived, Judge Thaddeus Clarke and Dr. Alpheus Grant, a prominent local physician, they received no answer to their knock. The door swung open, and they spotted Chalmers lying on the floor of the entryway of his home.

Dr. Grant dashed inside to try to assist Chalmers but quickly ascertained that he had been shot through the heart.

In an exclusive interview with the Claremont Beacon, Dr. Grant stated that he believed the murder must have taken place very shortly before they arrived.

"There were signs when I examined the body that indicated he had passed very recently," the doctor said. "Thankfully, he would not have lingered. It all happened very suddenly."

Sheriff Barlow says he will not rest until Chalmers's killer is brought to justice. "This is a horrific crime, a blight on our wonderful Claremont, but it is made even more horrific by the fact that this was an attack on a serving law enforcement offi-cer. Mark my words, this killer will hang."

In the meantime, Barlow stated that he believes Clare-mont remains safe for residents. Early evidence, he says, points to this being related to a criminal investigation with which Chalmers was assisting.

The investigation into the murder is ongoing. Rest assured, dear reader, that the Claremont Beacon will keep you apprised of any further developments.

Philip turned to me with an odd expression on his face.

"What?" I asked.

"The victim—that deputy sheriff, Adam Chalmers—is the person Jasper Reed was accused of murdering."

A chill ran down my arms. "So Jasper may have read this article and run away because he was afraid he'd get caught?"

"Possibly," Philip said. "I've read other newspaper accounts from this period. The sheriff seemed convinced Jasper was the killer, but some were skeptical."

"Well, if he was guilty, that's pretty unsettling." I pulled my arms close to my body and ran my hands over them. "Having a murder take place shortly after I arrive here and then learning a former owner of the property might have been a killer is a lot to take in." If I were superstitious, I might even wonder if the place was cursed.

"On the other hand, you've been here, what, a couple of weeks?"

"That's right."

"You've already found the storage spot under the stairs and this newspaper clipping," Philip said. "Who knows what else you may find out about Jasper or about the treasure?"

He was right. And I was too curious to be deterred.

If there were more secrets hidden in the inn, good or bad, I wanted to find them.

Chapter Thirteen

WHEN KATE and I stepped into Shannon's Bookshop the next afternoon, I saw that the front of the store was a coffee shop. The smell of freshly ground beans filled the air, and a selection of teas was displayed by the register, along with a small case of baked treats.

Off to one side, a cozy nook offered comfy couches and armchairs, all with lamps that could be angled to provide good light.

Beyond the coffee shop, rows of bookcases stretched deep into the store. The thought of all those stories, all that information, waiting to be read pulled me forward like a physical force.

Shannon stood behind the counter, smoothing back her light-brown hair, but I didn't see anyone else in the store. According to the plan Kate and I had discussed on the way over, we were here to casually chat with Shannon. We'd avoid accusations and direct questions about the murder.

And we'd shop a while before we spoke with her, so we'd look natural.

I gave Shannon a fluttery wave, and she waved back with a dimpled smile.

I moved toward the shelves like a moth to a fictional flame. Cozy mysteries, rom-coms, biographies, the occasional bestseller—I wasn't a picky reader. I just loved a story that offered escape, and Shannon's store was filled with options.

Before I knew it, I had three paperbacks tucked under my arm and was leaning against a shelf, reading the second chapter of a popular police procedural. It was only when footsteps passed one row over that I realized other shoppers were in the store.

"We know what we're looking for," a man's voice said.

"We want to browse a bit," a woman added.

"Take your time," Shannon called from the front.

I tucked the police procedural under my arm, caught Kate's eye, and headed for the register. We'd waited long enough for our conversation to seem casual.

"What a wonderful store!" I set my books on the counter and pointed to the display case. "I'll take these, one of those coconut macaroons, and a snickerdoodle."

"You've made some great selections," Shannon said, "both in books and cookies." Her blue eyes twinkled, and she rang up the first book.

"I didn't intend to shop today." I chuckled. "I got drawn in."

"Happens all the time," Shannon said. "For someone

who really loves books, there's nothing like the possibility of a new imaginary world to explore."

I nodded, and the thought zipped through my mind that, though Shannon was about twenty years younger than me, she and I thought alike. I forced myself to focus on the plan. "Mostly, we came in today because I wanted to apologize that I didn't get to talk with you very much at the reception."

"Not your fault at all. I feel bad that you wanted to meet people and instead had something so horrible happen at your inn." Shannon put my books and treats into a paper bag with twine handles and handed it to me.

"It was awful." I shifted my weight. "And everywhere I go, people tell me more gossip about J.B. and who might have killed him." I rolled my eyes. "It seems like everyone he knew had a reason to dislike him."

"He did have a rather ... prickly personality," Shannon admitted.

"Someone even told me you might have killed him because you were upset about a property he bought out from under you," Kate said.

Anger flickered in Shannon's eyes, then disappeared.

Holy cow, Kate. Direct questioning was not supposed to be part of our plan.

"The land by his restaurant?" Shannon said. "He outbid me. I might have been able to go a few thousand higher, but I was pretty much at my limit. He would have gotten the land in the end."

"He didn't even need it. It was selfish and mean." Kate

picked up an individually wrapped chocolate by the register and pulled out her wallet.

"You could certainly look at it that way." Shannon rang up Kate's chocolate, then scratched her nose. "When I heard his plans, I just tried to accept that it was his land and what he did with it was his business."

"A good attitude," I said, but it didn't match that flicker of anger I'd seen in her eyes. There was more to the story than she was telling. Since Kate had already waded in, we might as well try to learn as much as we could. "I'm sure that wasn't easy."

Shannon tipped her head and shrugged. "Getting back to the reception you held, I've thought a lot about that day. Someone on the patio pretty much had to be the killer."

"Well, it's not Lena, like that idiot Cal Granger thinks," Kate said.

"No." Shannon handed Kate her change and her chocolate. "I've never believed it was, and as I said, it wasn't me." Her jaw tensed, and she lowered her voice. "I think, if I had to pick a suspect—and I feel bad saying this—but I'd look at Rita."

"Rita?" Kate asked.

I pictured the smiling blond gift-shop owner. "What went on between Rita and J.B.?"

"It wasn't the two of them," Shannon said. "It was Rita's daughter, Kimberly, and J.B."

"Oh?" No one had mentioned a word about that, at least not to me.

Shannon leaned closer. "Kimberly graduated from high school this spring, and she wasn't sure what she wanted to do with herself. Rita suggested she get a job, save money, and take a year to get her bearings." Shannon made an awkward gesture with her hands. "Kimberly's sort of young for her age."

"I've known kids like that," I said. "A year of working sounds like a good idea."

"It might have been," Shannon continued, "except the job Kimberly took was waitressing at J.B.'s Steakhouse. Not a good fit for someone who's shy."

Kate and I exchanged glances.

"Kimberly would be the first to admit she wasn't a good waitress," Shannon said. "She'd get flustered and forget part of someone's order. Even telling people the day's specials was hard for her."

Kate bit her lower lip.

"Instead of gently talking with her and suggesting she might do better in the kitchen," Shannon said, "J.B. yelled at her, made her feel terrible, and fired her. No understanding, no second chances, no … heart."

Gosh, if someone had done that to either of my twins when they were eighteen, I'd have been furious. To be honest, I'd be furious even if it happened today when they were twenty-seven. "I guess for any mother, the Mama Bear response is automatic."

"Yeah, and from what I understand, the problem didn't go away. It spiraled into something worse," Shannon said. "Every time Kimberly considers another position, she's terrified to interview. If she manages to show up, she freezes."

"So more of the fallout from J.B. being a jerk could have occurred right before the reception. Seeing him there might have been too much for Rita," Kate said.

"Exactly," Shannon said.

"Did you tell all this to Detective Granger?" I asked.

Shannon shifted her weight from side to side. "I didn't. I mean, it wasn't as if Rita told me any of this herself. It's all just gossip, and I feel disloyal repeating it to the police if she's innocent. Oh, I wish I hadn't said anything. I feel terrible. I've known her all my life."

I could see her point, and I didn't want to create ill feelings with my fellow business owners, but I still thought the police needed to know. "Well, if I run into Detective Granger, I might mention it, but I won't tell him where I heard it."

"That sounds good," Shannon said.

I peeked into my bag, spotted the macaroon on top, and grinned at her. "This looks so yummy. I have a feeling I'll be back here often." Books and dessert were a powerful combination.

She waved, and Kate and I went back out onto the sidewalk along Lakeview Drive.

Rita's shop, Claremont Gifts, was two doors down on the way to where we'd parked.

"No better time than the present to talk to Rita," I said.

Kate agreed. "But did you notice how angry Shannon looked—just for a second—when I mentioned J.B.?"

I shot her a look. "You mean, when you went off-script and directly questioned her? What happened to playing it safe?"

Her face fell. "I'm sorry. I didn't mean to. I got carried away."

"It's okay," I said. "You're right. She did look mad for a second there. Maybe that business about calmly accepting that J.B. bought the lot she wanted was just an act."

Kate nodded. "For all we know, seeing that parking lot every day might have made her more and more mad."

"You may be right. On the other hand, Rita had to look out at his restaurant every day, at the place where her daughter had been treated so poorly." How had the man managed to irritate every person he came in contact with?

I repositioned my purse on my shoulder and took in Claremont Gifts' window display.

"Ooh, this looks nice." Every item in the window looked darling: tasteful sweatshirts, cute T-shirts, mugs with funny lake-vacation sayings, and plaques that I could picture in my house back in Kansas City.

I'd seen two Lakeview Drive businesses this afternoon and both were places I could wholeheartedly recommend to guests at the inn.

Kate pushed open the door and we walked in. Air-conditioned air washed over us, laced with a faint floral fragrance, but I didn't see Rita. Instead, a young woman who looked about twenty-five stood behind the desk putting price tags on boxes of notecards. Maybe Rita was in the back.

I turned to Kate. "Shall we look around?"

"Sure."

We wandered through the store. I did my best to look nonchalant and found two postcards, both with the same image of the lake, that were perfect for the twins.

I'd told Grace and Seth of my trip to Claremont for a few days in April and about how I'd ended up inheriting the inn from an elderly relation of their dad's and had come here to deal with the estate. I hadn't quite managed to tell them that I might decide to sell their childhood home and move to Claremont to run the inn. After all, I wasn't sure I would stay.

Neither of them lived at home anymore. Grace was married and lived in Vermont. Seth was an accountant in Boston, happily single. Still, it might be hard for them if I moved, so there was no need to upset them unnecessarily.

In the meantime, I liked to keep in touch. I'd sent lots of texts with photos, but one more image of beautiful Lake Claremont couldn't hurt if I did decide to move here permanently.

Eventually, Kate and I had perused the whole store with no sign of Rita. After a whispered discussion, we walked to the counter, and I handed my postcards to the salesclerk. "Is Rita here? We were hoping to chat with her."

The young woman's expression tightened, and she leaned toward us. "Are you friends of hers?"

"Known her for years," Kate said.

"I'm actually kind of worried," the salesclerk said. "She said she was going by the bank this morning, then to a doctor's checkup out of town. I thought she'd be back by now."

"Maybe things were really busy at the doctor's office."

"Maybe," the young woman said. "I expected her here sooner."

"Well, hopefully she'll arrive any minute now," Kate said.

I paid for my postcards, and Kate and I headed back to my car. All the while, my mind was racing.

When I'd met Rita at the reception, she'd seemed kind and warmhearted. Normally, I trusted my instincts. In this case, though, my instincts were telling me that none of the business owners I'd met was the killer, yet one of them had to be.

Somebody had me fooled, and it might have been Rita. "If you look at things from another angle, the fact that Rita went to the bank and left town could be seen as suspicious," I said slowly.

Kate turned to face me, eyes wide. "That's exactly what I was thinking."

"I'm going to text Addison and Philip and ask them to be on the lookout for her," I said. "If they see her around town, the doctor's office was probably busy. If no one sees her, well, it does make you wonder."

Maybe Rita wasn't as innocent as she appeared.

Chapter Fourteen

As soon as I got up the next morning, I promised myself I would return to Rita's gift shop right after lunch.

In the meantime, I refilled Tater's food and water bowls, folded two loads of soft, fluffy white towels and chatted with guests as I checked them out and made return reservations. I listened to a couple rave about Kate's pancakes with strawberry-kiwi topping. And I watched with amusement as a business traveler entertained Tater by projecting a beam from her laser pointer on the floor for him to chase. He raced after it, paws pounding the hardwood floor, and pounced, only to find his quarry gone.

Being part of the team at the Roseview Inn was beginning to feel more comfortable. In spite of the shadow of the murder that lingered, I felt a growing sense that Kate, Addison, and I might turn the place into a success.

About ten, when there was only one room left to check out, Addison came downstairs from where she had been cleaning. "I asked a bunch of people to let me know if they saw Rita." She held up her phone. "I got a text from a friend who says Rita is at The Griddle."

I must have looked confused.

"It's a breakfast place over on Bellamy Lake," Addison added.

"So she didn't leave the area yesterday."

"No," Addison said. "But my friend said she mentioned stopping by the gift shop this afternoon. Rita said today is her day off, and she wouldn't be there. After she ate breakfast, she was on her way to meet someone."

"That means if I want to talk to her, I need to catch her at the restaurant. The only guest left to check out has already made a return reservation and can simply leave her key on the desk. Do you think I have time to drive over to The Griddle before Rita would be finished and gone?"

"I would think so. She just ordered, The Griddle is notoriously slow, and it's only a forty-minute drive," Addison said. "I can handle anything that comes up while you're gone."

"That would be great. I'll help clean the rooms when I get back."

"It's a deal."

I called out my thanks and ran upstairs to get my purse. A couple of minutes later, I was about to dash down the stairs when a guest came out of her room.

"Hi Jessica," I said.

She caught my eye and gave a half-wave, but she looked stressed. Her narrow face looked incredibly tense, and her soft blond curls stuck out at odd angles as if she'd run a hand through them.

"Is everything okay?" I stepped closer.

"My dad's having surgery this morning in Cleveland. I have a business meeting I have to attend in Arkansas this afternoon, so I need to get on the road, but somehow, I've managed to lose my phone." She bounced a curled knuckle against her lips. "I've been over every inch of my room. It's nowhere. I guess I could stop by on the way back to get it, but I really want to get updates on my dad while I'm driving."

"Can you call it?"

"I put it on silent at night. I haven't turned that off yet." She shook her head. "Stupid, I know."

"Not stupid. You don't want to be woken up by some spammer." I patted her arm. In the lobby below, I could hear Addison helping a man check out and answering questions about things to do in the area before he and his wife drove home to St. Louis.

Sure, I could tell Jessica that Addison would help her once she was free, but that wasn't the type of hostess I wanted to be.

I'd probably miss talking to Rita, but this was more important.

"Let me help you look for your phone," I said. "Could you have left it somewhere on the first floor?"

"Maybe," she rubbed the back of her neck. "I'm so worried about my dad's surgery today that I don't feel like I'm thinking straight."

"I understand," I said gently. I'd been in situations like hers—times so difficult that I could look at something I was hunting for and not even see it. "Let's go through your morning, step by step. I bet we can find that phone."

Half an hour later, when we were making our second pass through the first floor, I spotted a pink phone case on a side table in the dining room. "Look!" I pointed.

Jessica let out a cry of relief and scooped it up. "Hold on." She quickly tapped the screen.

I stayed close, giving her privacy but wanting to be available if the news wasn't good.

But she looked up at me, eyes shining, cheeks curving into a big smile. "He's out of surgery. The doctor says it was a complete success!" She pulled me into a hug. "Oh, my goodness, thank you! You've been so kind."

"I was happy to help." It was true. This was a part of innkeeping that could fill my soul, caring for people, being needed.

She hugged me again and then dashed up the stairs, saying she needed to finish packing and get on the road.

I hurried up the stairs, where I heard Addison vacuuming on the second floor.

I popped into a room with the door open and a cleaning cart parked outside. "Is your friend still at The Griddle? Is Rita still there?"

"Let me check." Addison sent a quick text, then sighed. "Rita already left."

"Drat."

Addison glanced back down at her phone.

"Ugh, my friend said she heard Rita whispering on her phone—something about J.B."

I sighed. "That makes me wish I'd talked to her even more."

"I overheard you with that guest. You did the right thing, helping her," Addison said.

"I know. But I don't know how to find Rita if she's planning to meet someone rather than going to her shop." All I could hope was that she'd be back in her shop tomorrow and I could talk with her then.

Early that afternoon, when Addison and I had finished turning over the rooms, we were heading back downstairs when my phone rang. The caller ID read "Missouri's Finest Furniture."

I quickly picked up the call and learned the delivery van would be arriving in ten minutes. Our king-size mattresses, box springs, and simple bed frames would be arriving five days earlier than expected.

I told Addison, who ran to get Kate.

As I reached the first floor, I heard the loud *beep-beep-beep* of a backing truck.

Tater dashed toward the library, probably to hide under the couch.

But a zing of excitement shot through me, and I hurried out into the bright sunshine, where Addison and Kate soon joined me.

For most inns and hotels, the arrival of new mattresses was commonplace. For us, it was the beginning of a new direction, a direction we'd chosen together.

The truck backed up to the front entrance, and I silently thanked my lucky stars that the inn was empty until check-in. Next time I ordered anything large for the inn, I'd tell them ahead of time to deliver to the back.

Two guys hopped out, took a quick look at the guest room where I wanted the mattresses stored until the head-boards were finished, and walked toward the back of the truck. Inside, I could see the edges of the mattresses, all lined up, their plastic wrappings glinting in the sun.

The delivery guys lowered a ramp and started down it, carrying a mattress.

"Wait—" I glanced at Kate and Addison. They both looked worried.

"We're supposed to be getting king-size mattresses," I said to the delivery guys. "That looks too small."

They set the mattress down with a thump.

The older of the two guys hopped down, walked around to the front of the truck and came back with paperwork. "CozyPlush twins with matching box springs and twin-size dark oak frames."

He held out the paperwork.

My heart sank. The name, the address, and even my phone number were correct. The order wasn't.

Ten minutes later, after I called the store, Kate, Addison, and I went back inside. Addison left for the day. Kate returned to the kitchen. And the truck drove away, taking the mattresses with it.

Tater peeked out the doorway of the library as if to make sure that the beeping was finished. Seeing the coast was clear, he ambled over and nuzzled my legs.

"We won't get the right mattresses until next week, Tater." I sighed. The incorrect delivery had been as disappointing as reduced-fat potato chips. "It seemed like we were making progress. Now, it feels like I'm treading water." I scooped him up. "No progress on the mystery since I can't talk to Rita today, and no progress upgrading the rooms."

He purred loudly and butted my shoulder with his head until I rubbed between his ears.

He gazed up at me, eyes half-closed, and let out a loud, snorty purr—his ultimate expression of happiness.

Gradually, my disappointment melted away. It was hard to be sad when looking at his cute little ears and hearing that purr. He made me focus on the current moment, on the fact that he loved me, and not on a silly mix-up with an order.

"I guess it's really not that terrible, is it?" I said as I sat him down.

He nuzzled my legs again as if to say that life would be better if I forgot about mattresses and instead spent my time scratching his ears.

Perhaps it was time to show myself some grace. I was trying to learn a new career, renovate an inn, and solve a murder mystery.

Maybe each of those goals was something you achieved

in fits and starts, not in a steady progression of successful steps.

All I needed to do was to hang in there. Progress at learning inn operations would come. Progress on the renovations would happen. And progress on the mystery could be just around the corner.

Chapter Fifteen

Two hours later, none of the guests for the evening had shown up yet.

And I had run smack-dab into something that—if I decided to move permanently to Claremont and run the inn—I would have to figure out how to handle.

Sitting still drove me crazy.

Now that the new mattresses, pillows, and linens had been ordered, every task I thought of that needed doing would take me away from the desk. Most of them were even away from the inn. But guests could arrive at any time. I had to be there to greet them.

I considered playing Solitaire on the laptop. I did love games, but mostly because I played them with other people. A game alone wasn't the same.

Finally, my gaze landed on the stairwell. After I'd found the storage space under the stairs, I'd put the cups and saucers on display in the parlor. Not knowing what else to do, I'd ignored everything else—the empty cardboard box, the apple crate, the old wall sconce, the fraying umbrella, and the umbrella stand. I'd simply brushed the dust from my hands and closed the triangular door.

If I cleaned that space out thoroughly and maybe added some shelves, it would be useful storage. Because I'd only be a few feet from the desk while I was cleaning, I'd be available to greet guests as they arrived. I could even tell them how exciting it had been to discover a long-forgotten storage space.

I ducked into the laundry room and returned with the vacuum, a bucket of water, some rags, and a bottle of Murphy Oil Soap.

Tater wandered in from the parlor, ready to supervise.

I pressed the latch under the trim, opened the triangular door, and got to work. I had just returned from carrying the mouse-eaten cardboard box to the recycling bin at the side of the inn when Philip walked in.

"Hi, Philip. What brings you by?"

"I wondered if you had heard any more about Rita."

"Not a word. I'm going to go by her shop tomorrow afternoon. I thought she might have left town, but it doesn't sound like that happened."

He nodded and gestured toward the door to the space under the stairs, then to the vacuum. "Cleaning?"

"Yeah. I'm thinking we can put shelves under there. You'd be amazed how much storage it takes for the supplies for the inn."

"Would you like help moving things out?"

"Sure!"

He stepped into the storage space and came back out with the ancient wall sconce. "Looking at this makes me realize that more light would help if you plan to scrub the space. How about we set up a floor lamp in the hall?"

"That's a great idea. If you'll get one from the library, I'll go find an extension cord." A minute later, the storage space under the stairs was fully lit. It still smelled musty, but now I could see that the space even had baseboard trim. Horace must have asked the builder to include every bell and whistle, even in places visitors would never see. His home hadn't been about impressing the neighbors; it had been about experiencing the most gracious living possible.

With a good cleaning, the umbrella stand could be useful by the front door. I carried it to the laundry room. Philip took the remaining items to the carriage house and added them to the collection of odds and ends inside.

Back in the hall, we admired the space, and I was thinking how I would arrange shelves when I noticed something. In the far back corner, the dust and cobwebs looked thicker but—

"What's this?" I reached down to pull a piece of paper from where it was wedged between the baseboard trim and the wall. I brought it by the lamp and unfolded it.

Philip and I took a look. The ink on the page had faded to a rusty brown, the paper had yellowed, and the hand-writing was hard to read.

"Look at the bottom." A note of delight rang in Philip's voice. "It's a letter from Horace!"

"Holy cow!"

We exchanged glances and then read in silence.

Dear Mr. Gilman,

I write to acknowledge receipt of your estimate concerning the construction of a hidden room on the first floor of my residence. The proposed sum strikes me as fair, particularly in light of your esteemed reputation in St. Louis and your discretion in such sensitive matters. Your willingness to undertake the work unaccompanied and to speak of it to no one is greatly appreciated.

As discussed during your recent visit, accommodations and meals shall be provided during the duration of your stay. A commencement date of the 27th of May is agreeable, and I trust your journey here will be uneventful.

It will be a comfort to know such a refuge exists within my home, should past difficulties with certain laborers resurface.

Respectfully,

Horace R—

The signature was unfinished, and the ink trailed off the edge of the paper.

Electricity zipped down my spine, and I turned to face Philip. "Horace built a secret room? Not just a closet under the stairs, but a whole room? Oh, my gosh, that might be where the valuable item is!"

Philip pointed to what looked like a coffee stain on the bottom of the unfinished letter. "It appears as if he spilled something and then probably rewrote this."

"I'm glad he did. Otherwise, we never would have known about the secret room," I said.

Philip glanced around. "It's incredible to gain this insight into his life and to know that he had such conflicts with the miners that he built a place to hide. We shouldn't get too excited though. This inn has been renovated since Horace's time. The secret room could have been found years ago."

My shoulders sank. "You're right. I don't know much about what renovations have been done. Let's see what Kate knows. Hold on." I put up the sign on the check-in desk that said I'd be right back.

Philip and I took the letter to the kitchen, which smelled like cherries. A huge pot of what looked like pie filling sat on the stovetop.

"Kate, did Mrs. Everly ever tell you about a secret room Horace had installed on the first floor?" I asked.

"A secret room?" Kate turned from loading the commercial dishwasher.

I held out the letter for her to read.

Kate pushed back a wisp of hair and studied the page. "Geez Louise."

"Did the former owner ever talk about what renovations

had been done to the building?" Philip asked. "It was an inn before she bought it, right?"

"It was. They did work in the 1980s, including enlarging the kitchen," Kate said.

I looked around. That made sense. A private home wouldn't have had a kitchen this large at the beginning of the twentieth century.

"Mrs. Everly showed me the remodeling blueprints one time," Kate continued. "There wasn't any secret room that they took out."

"So it's still here?" My heart sped and I looked from Kate to Philip. "We simply need to find it, like we found the storage space under the stairs?"

"That's what it sounds like." Philip's eyes gleamed. "Think of what might be in there. The valuable item that Jasper hid, rare antiques, historic documents. Not to make it all about me, but this find could be incredible for my book."

"It really is exciting," Kate said slowly. An uncomfortable look passed over her face. "First we need to figure out who killed J.B., don't you think?"

"Of course." I should have realized that for Kate, whose sister might be charged with murder at any moment, the hidden room was nothing but a distraction. "As soon as Addison and I turn over the rooms tomorrow, I'm going to try again to talk to Rita."

"Thank you." Kate's eyes looked almost teary. "I'll go with you. In the meantime, I'd better finish up these cherry tarts."

"I need to get back to the lobby," I said. "Tonight's guests could arrive at any time."

Kate nodded, and Philip and I left the kitchen.

"I know you need to talk to Rita," Philip said. "But as soon as J.B.'s murder is solved, we should measure the outside of the inn and the rooms inside—"

"To look for Horace's hidden room," I finished. "This is so cool! I can't believe I inherited an inn with a secret storage space and a hidden room. I feel almost giddy."

"You're not alone. For a nerdy historian, this is unbelievable." He grinned at me.

"Nerdy, huh?" My description of him would have been more along the lines of *quietly handsome.*

"Nerdy is part of the job description," he said. "It might have even been in the contract I signed with the university. The history department has standards to maintain."

I chuckled and realized that it wasn't just excitement over the secrets of the inn that I was feeling. A sensation I almost didn't recognize hovered in my chest.

Oh, Philip was attractive—that was obvious. And the promise of innate kindness in his eyes was especially compelling. But that wasn't it exactly.

It was, I decided, a feeling of connection. Because I'd been thinking the exact same thing—that we needed to take measurements inside and out to find that room—before he even said it.

"I think you're right," I said. "We focus on the murder, but as soon as possible, we try to find the secret room. Next time I'm at the store, I'll get some graph paper so we can map things out and look for an inside space that doesn't match the outside measurements."

"Excellent," he said.

Our eyes met, and that odd feeling in my chest grew stronger.

More settled-in.

It's only a connection, I told myself.

Nothing more.

Chapter Sixteen

THE NEXT DAY, after Addison and I had cleaned the guest rooms and I'd eaten a quick lunch, Kate and I returned to Claremont Gifts, hoping to talk to Rita.

The bell on the door jingled as we stepped inside.

The day was even hotter and sunnier than the last time we'd visited the store, and I stood for a few seconds, soaking in the air conditioning and letting my eyes adjust to the lower light.

As before, Claremont Gifts offered a delightful selection of lake-themed items. This time, though, no one was at the counter, not even Rita's young assistant. I'd heard a rustle in the back as we walked in, but now … nothing.

"Hello?" I called out.

Kate and I stepped farther into the store, and each of us peeked down an aisle.

Halfway down my aisle, several Lake Claremont sweat-shirts had fallen off the shelf into a jumble of pastel fabric.

Unease pinched at my shoulders. Everything else I'd seen was perfectly in order.

As I rounded the end of the next aisle, I spotted more signs of trouble. A basket of beer cozies declaring "Life is Better at the Lake" lay on the floor. A ceramic statue of a frog holding a fishing rod had shattered into a half-dozen pieces on the tile. And at the end of the aisle, the toe of a white tennis shoe pointed toward the ceiling.

"Oh no! Kate, come here!" My heart pounded, and I dashed forward.

Rita lay on her back, a lidded carry-out cup tipped on the ground beside her. Her shirt had a rip near the shoulder, and there was a bloody wound on her head.

My chest tightened. Had she, like J.B., been killed? I knelt on the cool tile at her side and laid my shaking fingertips on her neck.

My breath came out in a whoosh. "There's a pulse," I told Kate.

"Rita." Kate gently jiggled her shoulder.

Rita's chest rose and fell, but she didn't come to.

I dialed 911 and reported the situation, explaining that Rita was alive but unconscious, and then held the phone so Kate could hear as well.

"You may be in danger," the operator said. "You should leave the store. Go out on the sidewalk where you can see other people."

I froze. "Do you think anybody else is in here?" I whispered to Kate.

For a moment, we were very still, listening as hard as we could.

Eventually, we both shook our heads. The store had that hollow feeling, the way my Kansas City office would feel when it was empty on the weekend.

But if the person who had done this to Rita had still been in the store, they could have heard me say she was alive. And they could come back. Ready to finish her off—or anyone else who stood in their way.

I couldn't abandon Rita, unconscious on the floor. "We can't leave her here defenseless," I told the operator.

I scanned the shelves around me. If I had to defend Rita—or myself—what could I use?

The umbrella decorated with images of fishing lures had a pointy tip, but it would probably only annoy someone, not disable them.

The snow globe with the gnome kayaking inside was heavy, but I wasn't sure how far I could throw it. If the attacker returned, I didn't want to deal with them at close range.

But the two wooden canoe paddles that had been intricately painted to use as decorative objects? They were perfect. I pointed to them, and Kate and I each grabbed one.

"Are you still there?" the 911 operator asked.

"Yes. I'm fine. I just wish I knew what to do for Rita."

"Help should be there any minute," she said.

"Good." I glanced back down at Rita and adjusted my grip on the wooden paddle. Any minute sure felt like a long time.

Eventually, the bell on the front door jingled and foot-steps entered the store. "Meredith? Are you in here?" Cal Granger's voice rang out.

I darted to the end of the aisle where he could see me. "Rita's unconscious. It looks like there was a struggle."

Behind him, two paramedics hovered at the door, each carrying equipment.

Cal stepped closer, his eyes narrowing as he saw Kate beside me and took in the paddles we each held. He pointed a thumb over his shoulder. "You two, go outside with them while I check the premises."

Go outside. The same advice the operator had given, but this time we wouldn't be leaving Rita alone. I set down my paddle and hurried toward the door.

The younger of the paramedics, a woman who looked about the age of my twins, pointed to a bench on the side-walk and walked over with us. "Why don't you all sit?" She looked us up and down. "Is either of you hurt in any way?"

We shook our heads.

I gratefully sank onto the bench. "Just a little frazzled."

She reached in her bag and handed us water bottles.

I unscrewed the cap on mine with a shaky hand and took a long drink. Then I scooted over on the bench, letting Kate sit in the shaded area too.

A few minutes later, Cal emerged from the store and told the paramedics they could go in. "It's empty, and I see signs that someone hurried out the back." He sat on the bench next to Kate and me and asked us to describe what had happened.

When we finished, his jaw tightened. "I don't like this. If I had to guess, I'd say the rustling noise you heard when you walked in was the person who attacked Rita, dashing out the back."

My stomach tensed.

"Detective?" The younger paramedic stuck her head out the door. "Rita's come to. She's quite disoriented though, and we're getting her ready to go to the ER."

Cal nodded, and she went back inside.

"My team should be here soon," Cal said to Kate and me. "I'm going to work with them to process the scene. Why don't you all go back to the inn and take it easy? Come into the station tomorrow to make a formal statement."

We agreed.

At this point, it sure seemed unlikely that Rita was the killer.

But we had no idea who was.

The next morning, I had just finished checking out a guest when Kate texted Addison and me and said she had news.

I set out my "Be Back Soon" sign and went to the kitchen, meeting Addison going in the kitchen door.

The sweet scent of cinnamon and butter filled the room, and I inhaled deeply. Today was French toast day.

"I texted one of Rita's neighbors," Kate said as she took a large pan of egg casserole out of the oven and set it on the stainless-steel island.

"Is she still disoriented?" Addison asked.

"Her neighbor said she's pretty fuzzy on what happened. Even so, I think one of us needs to stop by."

"I barely know her." I looked at Kate and Addison. "How about you?"

"I know her," Addison said. "She was my Sunday school teacher when I was in third grade."

"You could take her some flowers," Kate said.

"Pick some roses from the yard," I suggested. "If she's awake, see if she remembers what happened—not only yesterday, but also around the time of J.B.'s murder. I keep wondering if she was attacked because she saw something when he was killed."

"I'll go as soon as we finish the rooms," Addison said.

"Fingers crossed that she's regained her memory," Kate said, and I nodded.

For the rest of the morning, while I helped Addison clean, I kept thinking of Rita. If Detective Granger was correct, if Kate and I hadn't arrived at the gift shop when we did, the attacker would have had time to see that she was only injured. They might have struck another blow.

Rita would be dead.

The thought made me sick to my stomach.

Right before two, Addison and Kate finally knocked on the door of my suite, where I was finishing a late lunch of an egg salad sandwich. Addison said she'd been to the hospital.

I waved them inside and led them over to the couch and side chair in the sitting room.

"Does Rita remember anything about yesterday or the reception?" I asked as I sat down.

"Not a thing." Addison sat across from me. "She knows who people are and who she is, but the past week is all a blur. It really bugs her. She said she sort of remembers something about when she was attacked but she can't quite pin it down."

"She has no idea who hit her?" Kate asked.

"Nope, but the doctor told her it may come back."

"Otherwise, is she okay?" The memory of Rita, lying on the floor of her shop with me unable to help, was hard to shake.

"She seems fine. Says the hospital food could be improved." Addison scooted forward on the couch. "Here's the weird thing—her daughter was telling me all the people who've been by to see her. Most of them were people you'd expect, like her sister and the clerk at the gift shop. But Tony, Elliot, Vanessa, and Shannon have all stopped by."

My stomach tightened.

"All of our remaining suspects?" Kate asked.

"Every single one." Addison replied. "I mean, maybe they were simply being nice, or..."

"Or one of them could be wondering if she remembers the attack." I shifted my weight. "If they learn her memory could come back, they might try again."

Kate picked up her purse. "C'mon. We'll have a better chance of convincing Cal she's in danger if we talk to him in person."

"You're right," Addison said, "but I've got a homework

assignment due in"—she glanced at her phone and winced —"half an hour."

"I'll go with you, Kate." I wiped some egg salad off my fingers, gave Tater a pat, and the three of us headed out the door.

Kate and I took separate cars. Following her bright-red Mustang, I didn't have any trouble finding the police station.

We'd barely sat down in the uncomfortable plastic chairs in the lobby when the detective strolled out, said hello, and led us back to his office, a room that, except for a photo of an English bulldog on a shelf, was all business. A map of the county took up one wall, a clean whiteboard another.

He settled down behind a desk with three neat piles of papers and gestured to chairs facing him. "The desk sergeant says you wanted to talk with me before you make your statements?"

I adjusted my position in the chair. It was nearly as uncomfortable as those in the lobby and sat directly under an air-conditioning vent blowing icy air down the back of my shirt. "We're worried about Rita."

Kate leaned in and explained about Addison's visit to see Rita in the hospital and the guests Rita's daughter had listed. "Every single person who had opportunity to kill J.B. has been in to see Rita."

"We're afraid they might have tried to kill her to silence her and may be planning to finish her off," I added quickly.

"I'm way ahead of you," Cal said.

He was?

"Our newest officer, who just moved here from out of town, is standing at the nurses' station right near Rita's room, wearing scrubs."

I let out a heavy exhale. "Oh, that's wonderful. Do you know who attacked Rita?"

He sank lower in his chair. "No. I haven't nailed down the culprit yet, either for J.B.'s murder or for Rita's attack. If I had, I'd have brought them in for questioning." He shot an uneasy glance at Kate. "I have to tell you, Lena went in this morning to see Rita as well."

Kate jerked up taller. "Seriously, you can't still believe my sister is the killer. She's known Rita for years. I'm sure she went to see her at the hospital because she's nice. She probably made her special oatmeal chocolate chip cookies and took Rita some."

Cal held up a hand. "I'm not arresting Lena, but I can't ignore the evidence."

Kate's jaw tightened and her words poured out, fast and sharp. "I could almost understand why you suspected her initially, but you've had time to investigate. You need to wake up and realize Lena is not the killer!"

He crossed his arms over his chest. "She had as much opportunity to kill J.B. as the people you're suspecting. She had motive. She found the body. Like the others, she visited Rita this morning. And—" He paused dramatically. "She has no alibi for the time of Rita's attack. She says she was home alone eating lunch."

Sympathy flickered in my chest. His points made sense, and he was trying to stay professional. He couldn't ignore

Lena as a suspect just because he knew her. He probably knew almost everyone in town.

Kate sniffed. "I'm glad you're keeping an eye on Rita, but this conversation is hopeless. You'll never find the real killer if you're still focused on Lena."

I looked back at Cal. Maybe he didn't have the same level of intuition I had. Or maybe people were more close-mouthed when talking to the police. But he was trying to solve the case and protect his community. Look how he'd already asked Lena about her whereabouts at the time Rita was attacked.

Also, I got the sense that if an idea was presented—perhaps in a less imperious fashion than Kate's pronouncements—he would listen.

Which meant that, if we were going to find J.B.'s killer, I needed to come up with a clue that Cal couldn't ignore.

Chapter Seventeen

WE ONLY HAD one guest checking out the next morning, so the housekeeping chores were light. As soon as Addison and I had finished turning that room over and refreshing the others, she beckoned me to follow her to the kitchen, where she and Kate told me they were taking me out to lunch.

"You've been amazing." Kate put a tray of cinnamon rolls, ready to bake the next morning, into the commercial refrigerator. "Not just the fact that you're picking up the inn's operations so quickly and working so hard to update the place, but also that you're trying to help Lena. It really means a lot."

"Have you been to Pete's BBQ?" Addison asked. "The place on the water right past the marina?"

"No." I'd seen it but not eaten there. "Is it good?"

Kate and Addison exchanged disbelieving glances.

"You'll have to wait and see." Addison's eyes twinkled.

I was touched that they wanted to take me out, so I told myself not to be snobbish about slow-cooked meat. I was a Kansas City native. As anyone in the metro area could tell you, KC served the best barbecue in the world.

Maybe though, for around here, Pete's BBQ was considered tasty.

"That sounds wonderful," I said. "Just let me run upstairs to get my purse."

When we arrived, we found the restaurant packed, with all the indoor tables full. We squeezed into what was meant to be a two-top on the upper level of the outdoor patio. Despite the oversized umbrellas, nearly every diner wore sunglasses and a hat to combat the reflections off the water.

While we waited for our lunch, we discussed the suspects once more. Sadly, we didn't come to any brilliant conclusions, simply rehashed the same names: Tony, Shannon, Vanessa, and Elliot.

Half an hour later, I felt a twinge of guilt. As a loyal Kansas City gal, I couldn't actually admit out loud that Pete's brisket was the best I'd ever eaten. Or say that the steak fries were the absolute perfect level of crispiness or that the coleslaw should be featured on some cooking show on TV.

Maybe it was because we were eating lakeside, watching sunlight dance on the water. Or the fact that the restaurant was playing my favorite music, '80s dance hits, on its sound system. Or how touched I was by the "Roseview Inn" bumper sticker that Addison gave me, saying she and Kate both had one, and I should too.

So, no, I couldn't be disloyal to Kansas City, but I could tell them how much I'd enjoyed my lunch.

"This has been so yummy." I gestured to my plate, scraped clean of every bite. "I can't tell you how nice it is that you all wanted to take me out." I rested a hand on the bumper sticker. "You've both been so welcoming and have really made me feel like part of the team."

"We're really glad you came to Claremont," Addison said.

"It's like you've always been a part of things," Kate added.

A ripple of happiness swept through me, and I reached out and squeezed each of their hands. I felt appreciated and needed, exactly what I'd always wanted.

Oh, there was a downside to wanting to be needed. I knew myself well enough to realize that if my contributions were ignored, I could feel hurt. I did have a sensitive side that could get stepped on. But I didn't see that happening with Kate and Addison. They seemed like people who could be not just co-workers but caring friends.

The three of us smiled softly at each other, and then we all seemed to realize at the same time that our table was in high demand.

"Do you mind if before we go back, we pop across the street to Shannon's Bookshop?" Addison asked. "Grandpa wanted me to get a new thriller for him."

Kate and I readily agreed. I'd never turn down a trip to the bookstore.

A few minutes later, we walked in, waved to Shannon at

the desk, and after splitting up to wander a while, regrouped to browse a table of bargain hardbacks near the back of the store. Addison had picked up the thriller for her grandpa, Kate carried two cookbooks, and I'd found a book on Claremont's history written by a local author.

As we compared our finds, we overheard two women chatting one aisle over in the romance section. At first, I barely noticed them, but then the one with the higher-pitched voice started whispering.

"I can't believe I'm telling you this here of all places," she said, "but I think I know who killed J.B. Hodges."

My ears perked up, and I laid a finger over my lips and gestured with my other hand to Kate and Addison.

"Who?" the other woman in the next aisle whispered.

"Shannon!" the first woman replied. "I heard all about it from someone I golf with."

My pulse picked up, and Kate, Addison, and I exchanged glances. Quickly, using a combination of gestures and mouthed words, I asked them to go distract Shannon at the front of the store while I stayed to hear the rest.

Kate and Addison moved toward the front. I pretended to look at the bargain hardbacks, sliding around to be on the side of the table closest to the women in the romance section.

"So don't leave me hanging," the second woman whispered. "Why on earth do you think Shannon Lenox killed J.B.? She's always so nice that I find that hard to believe."

"Because," the first woman said, "my friend was

walking her dog right before she went to bed two nights before the murder. She saw Shannon sneaking along the side of J.B.'s house like she was coming around from the back."

"Maybe she'd been visiting with him on his back patio and was walking toward her car?" The second woman didn't sound convinced.

"My friend said it was a Tuesday night, so J.B. was at his restaurant. Shannon was acting ... what's the word she used? Furtive. That's it. Like she had been doing something she didn't want anyone to know about."

"If it was almost bedtime, wouldn't it have been dark? I bet if your friend saw anyone, it wasn't Shannon."

"There was a full moon," the first woman insisted.

The second woman snorted. "I still don't believe it. Even if—and I have my doubts—your friend saw Shannon near J.B.'s house, that doesn't mean she's a killer. For all we know, she was looking for her cat."

"Shannon doesn't live anywhere near J.B."

"I'm not listening anymore. Shannon's a nice person, not a killer." The second woman sounded a little miffed, and I heard her walk off.

I slipped away, taking each step carefully so my tennis shoes would make as little noise as possible, and wound my way through the self-help books toward the front. No need to have either woman realize I'd been eavesdropping.

At the front counter, Shannon handed Kate a vanilla frappé and rang up my purchases nice as could be. The whole time, my mind raced. As soon as I was outside with

Kate and Addison, I told them what I'd heard. "It sounds suspicious."

"I agree," Kate said.

"For all we know," Addison said, "Shannon could have planned to wait for J.B. in his house and kill him there. When she couldn't find a way in, she killed him at the reception."

I tipped my head in agreement. "It seems far-fetched, but why else would she sneak around his house at night?"

"Look." Kate pointed back toward the bookstore. "Those other women are leaving. It's the perfect time for us to go talk to Shannon and get to the bottom of this."

Addison and I looked at each other, then nodded.

"There are three of us," Addison said.

"And we want answers," I added.

We doubled back to the bookstore.

Shannon looked up as we walked back in. "Did you forget something?"

"Actually, we wanted to talk with you." I looked around. "Do you have any other customers here?"

She shook her head slowly, and her shoulders stiffened.

I moved closer to the counter. "When we talked a few days ago, you acted like you'd accepted the fact that J.B. bought the lakefront property you wanted, only to build an unnecessary parking lot. Like you were fine with it. That wasn't true, was it?"

Shannon shrugged. "I mean, forgiveness, acceptance... Things like that are always a work in progress."

"You need to stop lying, Shannon." Kate crossed her

arms over her chest and glared at her. "We know you killed J.B."

"I did no such thing," Shannon said quickly.

I stepped closer. "So explain why you were seen sneaking around his house when he wasn't at home a few nights before he was murdered."

Tension spread from Shannon's shoulders to the rest of her body. Even her hands looked rigid. "Why would you say that?"

"Someone saw you. It was a full moon, so it was easy to recognize you, and easy to see that you looked guilty of something."

Shannon drew her lips in.

I stayed silent, looking at her, and Kate and Addison joined me in a wall of accusation. If she was the murderer, it was time for her to come clean.

Above us, a ceiling fan clicked softly with each rotation. With every click, Shannon bit her lower lip harder.

Suddenly, her eyes teared up. "I know it was wrong, and I've felt guilty every day since I did it."

My pulse sped. We'd done it. We'd found the killer. I reached out and patted her arm. "You'll feel better if you tell us everything."

"What he did just seemed so unfair," Shannon continued. "I wanted to do something—even if it was only a little thing—to get back at him for buying that land out from under me."

Kate's words exploded out. "Killing him and letting my sister take the blame is not a little thing!"

Shannon shook her head so violently that her hair whipped from side to side. "You've got it all wrong. I didn't kill J.B.—I killed his tomato plants."

My shoulders fell. "His tomato plants?"

"He had these six tomato plants in containers on his back deck. Practically every time I was around him, he went on and on about how he'd ordered special seeds from online and he was going to have the sweetest, freshest cherry tomatoes any time he wanted them. So one night when I knew he'd be at work, I snuck onto his back porch, sprinkled herbicide around the base of each plant, and used water from his watering can to dissolve it."

"That's what you feel guilty about?" Addison said. "Not murder?"

Shannon shook her head again. "Not murder."

A strange flicker of understanding passed through my brain. I'd seen this back in the office in Kansas City. Oh, nobody there poisoned anyone's plants, but I'd seen how a feeling of injustice could push a person to a small, private rebellion. Like the time one of the secretaries kept hiding the umbrella of a vice president who belittled her.

"I justified it by telling myself he didn't have pets, and the herbicide wouldn't have hurt him if he'd come in contact with it. It was only bad for plants," Shannon said. "But it was a horrible thing to do, the only time in my whole life I've ever done anything that even came close to criminal. My sister talked me into—" She stopped. "It was my fault and mine alone. I'm sorry I didn't tell you the whole truth." She raised her eyes to meet mine.

"Your lies make you look guilty of killing him," I said.

"I didn't. I swear," she whispered.

"The only way to make this right," Kate said, "is for you to tell Cal Granger what you did."

Shannon's eyes grew huge. "Do I have to?"

Kate planted her hands on her hips. "If you don't tell him, I will."

"O-okay." Shannon's voice wobbled. "I hope he believes me when I tell him that's all I did." She turned to me. "Please believe me, Meredith. I hate that I just met you and lied to you. It's not who I am. I…" She glanced down.

I gave her a sad smile, then turned toward the door and walked out with Kate and Addison. I didn't like to hold grudges, and it wasn't as if I was the police. She didn't owe me any explanation at all. Still, I didn't like to be lied to.

On the sidewalk, Kate turned to Addison and me. "I don't care what she says about tomatoes, I still think she did it. She lied about one thing, so she's lying about the other. Plus, I bet there would be physical evidence at the scene that would link her to the crime."

I exchanged glances with Addison.

Sadly, it was all too easy for Kate to jump to conclusions when the police were focused on her sister.

"I don't know, Kate," Addison said slowly.

"Yeah," I said. "I think this time Shannon was telling the truth. She killed the tomato plants, but someone else killed J.B."

Kate's face fell.

Addison let out a long sigh. "And we have no idea who."

For a few seconds, we walked along in silence, our footsteps dragging.

Halfway down the block, I stopped and turned to them. "You know what? I know one more place we can look for clues."

Their eyes lit, and I told them my idea.

Chapter Eighteen

ADDISON and I had fluffed the last pillows and smoothed out the tiny wrinkles in the pillowcases when Kate burst into Room 8, phone held high like a victory flag.

"You were right, Meredith. It took a while, but I searched on social media like you suggested, and I found a clue!"

We'd decided since I was new to the area and Addison was too young to have much interest in the social media sites our suspects might have used, that Kate was the person to do the search. She was friends online with all of our suspects and their friends as well.

"What did you learn?" Addison asked.

"Look at this." Kate held her phone toward us, showing a post from someone I hadn't met, a guy named Plank Wilson.

"Plank?" I looked up at Kate. That was an unusual name.

"He's a carpenter. His dad's a carpenter. Started working with him when he was in high school, right about the time he shot up about a foot in one school year. At the time, he was six foot two and maybe 150 pounds."

"Now he's more like 300," Addison said. "Look what he posted."

PLANK WILSON: *Well, don't forget Tony. He always said nobody crossed him without paying for it—and look what happened to J.B.*

Kate pointed to the screen. "It's posted the same day as the murder."

I stared down at it. She was right. "The whole discussion seems to be about revenge."

"It is," Kate said. "Sort of. It started out as one person saying someone else needed to stand up for themselves."

"Do you think that's what Plank means?" Addison's face twisted up. "I'd think if he knew Tony was the killer, he'd have told the police."

I turned to Kate. "Do you know Plank well? Could you message him and ask what he meant?"

"I tried," she said. "No reply, and it looks like he hasn't been online in a day or so."

Addison held up a finger, her eyes narrowed as she stared past us. "Let me think a minute…"

Kate and I stood there, silent. Addison looked like one of my twins, trying to remember the forms of a Spanish verb the night before a test.

Addison raised her arms in victory. "Got it. I knew I'd seen the truck for Wilson's Carpentry somewhere yesterday. It was at DeeAnn Davis's house over on Willow Street. It looked like he was redoing her porch steps."

"Let's go talk to him!" Kate said.

"We've got one more room to turn around," Addison said.

"But we'll do our best to be quick," I added. "When I talked with Tony, I rather felt like I'd found a friend in the industry. If he's the killer and was lying to me the whole time, I want to know about it. Now."

An hour later, Kate turned her car onto a quiet street and parked in front of a green Craftsman-style bungalow. A white Ford pickup truck with "Wilson Carpentry" and a phone number painted on the door was parked in the driveway.

A heavyset man was using a circular saw between sawhorses under a wide maple tree, but the tree's shade was no match for the heat and humidity of southern Missouri in June. Sweat dampened bits of strawberry-blond hair that stuck out under his ball cap.

Earbuds stuck out of his ears and when he wasn't using the saw, he moved in time with a beat only he could hear as he shifted new boards into position.

We climbed out, immediately engulfed in the humidity. Today was a scorcher.

Kate walked into his line of sight and waved.

He pulled out his earbuds, withdrew a phone from his front pocket, and tapped the screen. "Kate, good to see you." He turned and spotted Addison and me. "You too, Fincheroo. Who's this?" He smiled at me.

"Plank, meet Meredith Whitfield, the new owner of the Roseview Inn," Kate said. "Meredith, this is Plank Wilson."

I said hello.

"Pleased to meet you." Plank wiped his fingers on his jeans, inspected them, and reached out to shake my hand. "If you all are here to see DeeAnn, she's at her sister's this week. Didn't want to listen to me hammering."

"No," Addison said. "We came by to ask you a question."

Plank blinked but spread his hands wide. "Ask away."

"Meredith's trying to figure out who killed J.B. Hodges. You know, since he was killed at the inn," Addison said. "Kate and I've been helping her."

"Cal Granger's being an absolute fool." Kate rolled her eyes. "He thinks Lena's the murderer."

Plank shifted his weight back onto his heels. "Yeah, I heard that. Seems crazy to me. I went through school with Lena. She's ... well, she's not got your gumption, Kate. If some guy cheated on you, you'd probably whack him up aside the head with a cast-iron skillet."

Kate snorted. "You know me well, Plank. But you're also right about Lena, which is why we're here." She explained about the social media post she'd seen online.

He brushed some sawdust off his cheek. "Nah, that wasn't about the murder."

"But you were talking about Tony seeking revenge on J.B.," I said.

"I was, but Tony wouldn't kill nobody." Plank hooked his thumbs in his back pockets.

"What did he do?" Addison asked.

"I guess I should think before I spout off online, shouldn't I?" Plank stretched his shoulders.

"Plank," Kate said, "you ignored my text message, and we drove all the way over here…"

He kicked at a tuft of grass. "It's not really my place to tell you, but I guess it's better than letting you think Tony's a murderer."

The three of us leaned in.

"When Tony learned his wife was sleeping with J.B., he had a big group staying at Bellamy Pointe, maybe thirty people there for a family reunion. He overheard them talking about reservations they'd made for dinner at J.B.'s. After they went out on the lake, he called and, disguising his voice, canceled the reservation."

"Ooh, that's mean," Kate said.

"When they came back to Bellamy Pointe all upset because there was no space for them at J.B.'s, he pretended he'd pulled it together at the last minute, but he had a private room already set up in the hotel restaurant."

"Sneaky," Addison said.

"Yeah, Tony's a pretty slick guy. I bet J.B. got some nasty reviews online after that," Plank said.

I bet he had.

Like Shannon killing J.B.'s tomato plants, Tony had

exacted a small amount of revenge. His action probably wasn't even serious enough to be considered a misdemeanor, but it had been a definite way of striking out in retaliation.

Because, like Shannon, he'd been mad.

J.B. had made a lot of people mad.

Kate looked at Plank. "You really don't think Tony's the killer?" Disappointment rang in her voice.

"Nah, not Tony."

Her head drooped, and she rubbed the toe of her tennis shoe against the concrete driveway. "We've got to figure out who did this. I can't let Lena end up in jail."

"I'd like to help you, Kate, but..." Plank pressed his lips together and shifted his lower lip from side to side, like someone trying to evenly spread a layer of Chapstick. "Ah, heck, I hate to say this. I mean, he and I were sort of friends back in school..."

Kate's head shot up. "You suspect someone else?"

"I did overhear something. And with the way you all are digging, if you don't hear it from me, I guess you'll hear it from someone else."

Kate stepped closer. "What?"

"Apparently, J.B. held the loan on Elliot's gallery, and Elliot missed a few payments," Plank said. "J.B. told him if he didn't make things right, he'd take him to court. There was a good chance Elliot would lose the place."

"Oh, that's harsh," Addison said. "The gallery is his whole life."

"I know," Plank replied. "And if Elliot doesn't have

money to pay his mortgage, he probably doesn't have the money to move his business somewhere else."

"So we should look more closely at him," I said. "Maybe we should stop by his art gallery and ask a question or two and—"

"Hold on there," Plank said. "If Elliot killed J.B. and attacked Rita, you shouldn't be questioning him. You don't want to be next."

Kate, Addison, and I exchanged glances.

Kate pulled out her phone. "Well, it's later than I thought. I've got to get back to prep for teatime."

"And I've got an online exam in an hour," Addison said.

I, on the other hand, wasn't expecting anyone to check in for more than two hours.

Maybe, if I asked Philip to go with me, I could stop by Elliot's gallery and talk to him. Not outright accusing him, but perhaps indirectly learning if he had an alibi for the time when Rita was attacked.

He may have been telling the truth earlier—that he hadn't been angry about the amount of money he lost to J.B. in the poker game; he'd been angry because the guy was cheating.

But losing his gallery was a much bigger financial hit.

A hit that might be a motive for murder.

Chapter Nineteen

As soon as we returned to the inn, Addison hurried home to take her online exam and Kate dashed to the kitchen. Before I sent a text to Philip to see whether he could join me in stopping by Elliot's gallery, I needed to change out of my tennis shoes. They were great for housekeeping, but too hot for the rest of the day.

I climbed the stairs to the second floor and unlocked the door to my apartment. On the floor, just inside the door, was a folded sheet of paper.

A complaint from a guest perhaps? Or maybe a compliment? Or would they even know that the unmarked door led to my personal quarters?

I picked up the paper.

Tater opened one eye from where he'd been sleeping on the couch.

"C'mon, Tater, sit with me while I see what this is."

He closed both eyes and ignored me, and I settled down

into the upholstered chair as I unfolded the paper and scanned the words on it.

STOP POKING YOUR NOSE INTO J.B.'S MURDER. IF YOU DON'T, YOU'LL END UP JUST LIKE HIM.

Ice shot through my veins. I placed the note on the coffee table as if it were a bomb, then stared at it.

It was written on regular, 20-pound bond paper like you'd put in a copier or a printer and typed in plain black ink in what looked like Times New Roman font. If I had to bet, the paper had no fingerprints on it. But it had the faint smell of —I sniffed more closely—something I couldn't quite identify.

I'd smelled it before, but ... no idea.

Whatever that smell was, the person who had left the note had walked right into the inn, known where the owner's suite was, and come up to the second floor. Besides that, they had presumably known that Kate, Addison, and I had all been out of the inn.

My stomach slowly froze into a ball.

Before today, this mystery had seemed, well, much further removed. Like as long as I took someone with me, I could carefully ask questions of a suspect and still be safe.

Now all I could think about was the fact that if we had a night with no guests, I'd be at the inn alone.

I didn't feel like being Jessica Fletcher anymore. I felt ... scared.

Should I call the police?

If I did, I'd have to explain to Cal Granger what I'd been doing, and he wouldn't be at all pleased.

No, what I needed was to talk this over with my friends. But Kate would be slammed getting ready for teatime, and Addison had an exam to take.

I grabbed my phone and sent a text to Kate, Addison, and Philip, telling them there had been a development and we needed an emergency meeting. Within minutes, they'd all replied, and we arranged to meet at the staff fire pit overlooking the lake after dinner.

I set my phone on the table well away from the note, went over to the couch, and scooped up a sleepy Tater. I carried him back to my chair, positioned him on my lap, and held him close.

"Oh, Tater," I whispered. "What have I gotten myself into?"

By eight that evening, I was calmer. I'd checked in four guests. I'd watched an old episode of *Friends* while I ate dinner. I'd talked through with Tater why I would be safe, even if the inn was empty. I'd lock the doors to the outside, and I had my own key to the owner's quarters to provide an extra layer of protection.

Plus, I'd decided that the note would make me wise up. Before today, I'd foolishly thought I was safe conducting my investigation. I'd believed no one felt threatened by my casual questions. Now I knew differently. Now I'd be on alert.

I squared my shoulders and headed out to the back patio and down the path to the staff fire pit.

Addison was already there, sitting in one of the four chairs arranged in a circle. The humidity had dropped some, so it was less sticky than it had been in the afternoon, and looking at the lake somehow made me feel cooler.

Philip appeared from around the dogwoods and took the chair next to me, across from Addison. "Have we discussed the 'big development' yet?"

"I was just about to ask," Addison said.

"Wait for me," Kate cried, sliding into the remaining chair across from me.

"This is what I wanted to discuss." I pulled out the note, which I'd put in a sealed plastic bag. "Someone slipped this under the door of my apartment while we were out this afternoon." I turned to Philip and added, "The owner's quarters are behind an unmarked door on the second floor."

I passed the note to Addison, who read it, then covered her mouth.

Kate took it from her and held it so both she and Philip could see it.

Philip's jaw tightened, but he remained silent as he handed the note back to me.

"Really trying to scare you, weren't they? Letting you know that they know exactly where you sleep." Kate pursed her lips. "Whoever did this is a real threat."

"What did Cal Granger say?" Addison asked.

"I, uh…" I stared at my shoes. "I haven't told him yet."

Philip turned toward me. "Why not?"

"Well, he's not going to be pleased if he learns how much I've been snooping." My decision had seemed logical earlier, but Philip was looking at me as if he strongly disagreed. "And I wanted to talk to the three of you first."

"You have to tell him," Kate said. "He needs to dust the note for fingerprints."

Yeah, I'd thought of that, which is why I'd put it in a plastic bag, but I didn't hold out much hope. "Don't you think that if the killer was smart enough to sneak into the inn when we all were gone, they'd be smart enough to wear gloves?"

"Maybe," Addison said. "You can't know that, though. There might be a hair or a fiber from something they were wearing that would be a clue."

"You don't want to obstruct the investigation," Philip said.

I hadn't thought of that.

"Hey." I opened the plastic seal on the bag and held it toward Kate. "What does that smell like to you?"

She took the bag and sniffed. "Hazelnut coffee."

My chest grew tight, and I felt my eyes widen.

Philip leaned over and sniffed the bag as well. "I agree. Hazelnut coffee."

"Holy cow," I said. "That's what Elliot offered me when I talked with him last week at his gallery."

"Well, you can't talk to Elliot now," Addison said. "Not even if you take Philip with you, like you were thinking."

"Elliot?" Philip leaned forward. "Did you discover something new about him?"

"We sure did," Kate said.

I explained what we'd learned and how I'd considered asking him to go with me while I casually talked to Elliot to see if he had an alibi for the time when Rita was attacked. "Of course," I said slowly, "that was before I got the note."

Philip's eyebrows drew together. "That makes the note even more threatening. I strongly advise you to stay away from Elliot."

"I agree," Addison said. "Let Cal talk to him."

They were right. "I'll go to the police station first thing in the morning."

"Would you like me to go with you?" Philip asked. "Or stay in a guest room at the inn tonight?"

"No. I'll be okay. We've got four guests in the building, one right across the hall from me." I turned to Addison. "Can you handle any issues at the inn starting around 7:45 tomorrow morning? I'll go talk to Cal and then help you with the rooms."

"Sure thing." Addison touched my arm. "You've been really brave, but it's time to let the police handle this."

"She's right," Kate said. "Surely, with this note, Cal will understand that you're getting close to the truth, and he needs to listen."

I nodded and stared out over the sun's last rays reflecting off the lake. "First thing tomorrow, I'll talk to him."

Chapter Twenty

THE NEXT MORNING, with Addison keeping an eye on things at the inn, I walked into the Claremont police station.

I gave my name to the officer at the desk and took a seat in one of the hard plastic chairs in the waiting area. I was halfway through reading a poster on avoiding internet scams when Cal appeared in the doorway and called me back to his office. As before, the space was extraordinarily tidy and devoid of personal items except the photo of a dog.

"That's a nice-looking bulldog," I said. Maybe a short chat about his pet would make him less annoyed when I admitted I'd been snooping.

Instead of the smile I'd expected, pain flickered through Cal's eyes. "Thanks. That's Sparkplug. I lost him two weeks ago."

My mouth went dry. Drat. The last thing I wanted to do was to make the man dwell on his loss. "I'm so sorry."

He glanced away, then looked back to me, his face composed. "What brings you in today?"

My stomach knotted but I forced myself to go on. Quickly, I explained that when I returned to the inn yesterday afternoon, I'd found a note in my apartment there. I pulled the plastic bag from my purse and slid it across the desk to him.

"I touched it at first," I said. "It was folded, and I thought it was a note from a guest."

His eyes narrowed as he read it, and he looked up at me. "What exactly have you been doing?"

Haltingly, I listed all the people I'd talked to.

The longer I spoke, the tighter his jaw grew.

"I'm sorry," I finished. "I didn't realize how much I was putting myself at risk."

"Why are you just telling me about this today?"

The knot in my stomach grew. "I, uh, I was sort of afraid you'd be mad at me."

"Well, I'm not happy, that's for sure. It's bad enough that J.B. was killed and Rita was attacked. I don't want something happening to you as well." He set the note aside. "I'll dust this for prints, but I'm not optimistic."

"Yeah, I'm not either," I said. "But I do think I know who the killer is."

"You do?" His chin rose. For an instant I saw how much the idea of a murder in his town weighed on him, then his eyes shuttered.

"I heard that J.B. held the loan on Elliot Renner's art

gallery and was taking him to court because Elliot had been missing payments. If Elliot's very livelihood was threatened, he could have killed J.B. If Rita suspected him, he could have tried to kill her too."

"But—"

I kept talking, determined to have my say. "When I visited Elliot's gallery, he offered me some of his favorite hazelnut coffee, which is what that note smells like."

There, I'd shown him the note, and I'd shared my theory. Of all the people I'd looked into, Elliot seemed the most likely suspect to me. If I was right, all Cal needed to do was to bring Elliot in and question him until hopefully he admitted what he'd done. Who knew? Maybe I was wrong. Maybe his fingerprints were even on the note, which would wrap things up nicely.

Cal shook his head. "Elliot's got an airtight alibi for the time of Rita's attack."

My stomach sank. "He does?" Hold on. I wasn't giving up. Alibis could be faked. "Maybe he got someone to lie for him."

"I don't think so, Meredith. The woman giving him an alibi isn't going to lie to me."

"Are you sure?"

"I'm sure. He was talking with my mom about an upcoming show featuring her paintings."

"Oh." His mom? Well, that destroyed my theory. "Do you still suspect Lena? Or do you have someone else in mind as the killer?"

He crossed his arms over his chest. "You do realize I could arrest you for interfering with an ongoing investigation, don't you?"

I swallowed. I hadn't even considered that. Holy cow, there was no way I could improve things at the inn if I was in jail, and what would I tell my kids?

But I couldn't back down now. "I'm sorry, but the murder did take place at my inn, and it's hurting my business."

His shoulders stiffened, and I got the distinct impression that I should have kept my mouth shut.

I sank down in my chair.

"I understand why you're concerned for your business, Meredith. And I appreciate that you want to help Lena because she's Kate's sister. Because of that, and because—despite the fact that she drives me crazy—I respect Kate, I'm cutting you some slack here."

I looked up hopefully.

"The answer is no," he said. "The bottom line is that every lead my team has followed up has gone nowhere. However"—he gave me a pointed stare—"that doesn't, in any way, mean you should keep playing amateur sleuth. This is murder we're talking about, and the killer has made it a point to warn you off. If you ignore that warning, what do you think is going to happen?"

The knot in my stomach edged into nausea.

Not sure what else to say, I mumbled a quick thank you, grabbed my purse, and headed back to the inn.

Along the way, I passed J.B.'s Steak & Seafood. It was shuttered and looking as if it was closed for good.

J.B. was murdered.

Rita had been attacked.

The killer had been right outside my owner's suite, angry that I'd been snooping.

And neither I nor the police had any idea who that killer was.

Early that afternoon, after three guests had checked out, I helped Addison finish turning over the rooms. Then I went to my quarters, ate a late lunch, and sat on the couch beside Tater, bringing each suspect to mind.

Elliot, the art gallery owner, had an alibi for the attack on Rita, but the note had smelled like hazelnut coffee, the exact thing he offered me at his gallery. Could he have killed J.B. and paid someone to attack Rita to confuse the police?

Vanessa, the real estate agent, had claimed her business wasn't hurt when J.B. bad-mouthed it. Even if that was true, it didn't mean that his words hadn't angered her.

Then there were two suspects who'd admitted they were angry and taken some sort of revenge. First, Shannon, the bookstore owner, who'd been so upset by how J.B. bought the lakefront property she'd wanted that she'd poisoned his tomato plants. She'd let that flash of anger show in her eyes.

She'd definitely been more annoyed with him than she'd let on.

And Tony, the hotel owner, whose wife had an affair with J.B. and who had sabotaged the reservation of a large party at J.B.'s restaurant. He had a strong motive and was smart, sneaky, and—as Plank described him—slick.

I slumped down against the back of the couch. Four suspects. One of them had to be the killer, but which one? I let out a loud sigh.

Tater's ears twitched, and his eyes cracked open.

"Sorry, fella. I didn't mean to wake you."

Tater stood, stretched, and moved to my lap.

"Aww, you're such a sweetheart." I scratched his back, and he began purring.

Together we sat, and I slowly felt the stress drain from my body. My mind eased and instead of the previous pressure I'd felt to identify the killer, the issue became more of a puzzle to solve. I thought and thought, examining each piece. At last, I realized something. It didn't seem like that big a deal, but maybe...

I texted Addison and Kate, and we met in the kitchen.

"I think I may have something," I said. "Of all the suspects, Vanessa was the only one who came to me to tell me that I shouldn't suspect her. Like she was keeping an eye on our investigation. Just like someone had to have been watching to know when we'd all be out of the inn so they could leave that threatening note."

"That seems like a stretch," Addison said.

"Maybe," I admitted. "But there was something about

Vanessa's body language when I talked with her at the bakery. I can't put my finger on it, but I think she was more tense than she was letting on." I glanced over at Kate. "Is there anything else you can think of about her and J.B.? You grew up here, and you're pretty close in age."

"Let me think..." Kate looked off to one side, brows drawn together.

After a moment, she turned back. "I did hear that back in high school, J.B. won the Pullman scholarship that Vanessa really wanted. For years, the family has given a full-ride scholarship to one student every year. The year J.B. won, he didn't even need it. His parents could have afforded to send him to college."

"Hers couldn't?" I asked.

"No," Kate said. "I once overheard someone ask her why she hadn't become a stockbroker, like she talked about. She said she couldn't afford college, and something about her family made her too nervous to take out student loans. She said selling real estate and handling property management was the best way she knew to make a decent living without a college degree."

"Oh, my gosh." I pulled out my phone.

"All that took place twenty years ago. Why would Vanessa kill J.B. now?" Kate asked.

"Look." I held up my phone, showing a real estate listing for a huge house, probably built about the same time as the inn.

"The Pullman place?" Kate said. "That's a new listing."

"When we were at the bakery, Vanessa mentioned she

just got it. What if when she talked with Madge Pullman about the listing, it reminded her about the scholarship, and that's what prompted her to kill J.B.?"

"Maybe." Kate ran a hand over her hair. "It still seems unlikely to me. Twenty years is a long time ago."

"It is." My shoulders sank. "I don't know how we could prove my theory anyway."

"If it's true," Addison said, "I think I might have a way to prove it."

"How?" Kate and I asked together.

"Madge Pullman is friends with my grandfather, and she's one sharp 85-year-old lady. She's moving to a retirement community north of town where they have a very competitive bridge club. Grandpa says she'll annihilate them."

A tingle of excitement ran down my spine. "So, if Vanessa remembered the loss of the scholarship and was angry about it, Madge might have picked up on it?"

"I think so," Addison said.

"Do you think Madge would talk to me?" I asked.

"Sure." Addison pulled out her phone. "I'll call Grandpa to get her number, then call her and ask."

I could only hear one side of Addison's conversation, but it was soon obvious that Madge would be happy to see me.

A moment later, Addison hung up. "She says as long as you'll ignore the fact that the house is a mess, she'd be happy to have you stop by. She's been out of town since right after she listed the house. A family member passed away."

"Are you sure it's okay to intrude on her grief?"

"Madge said her aunt was 102, had lived a really good life, and died peacefully in her sleep. She didn't seem that upset, and she said she'd be home all afternoon."

"Wonderful." I walked toward the door. "I'm headed there now."

Chapter Twenty-One

SURE ENOUGH, when I parked in the driveway of Madge Pullman's house, there was a sign in the front yard from Vanessa's real estate firm.

And, as Addison had said, Madge was happy to welcome me into her living room—a large space where all the upholstered furniture featured the same pink-and-green floral print.

The home was cool, quiet, and soothing. In contrast to what she'd claimed, it was not in any way a mess unless the three pieces of mail sitting on the hall table counted. Clearly, even with her upcoming move, packing the first floor had yet to begin.

"Please, have a seat." The tiny, white-haired woman gestured to a loveseat and settled herself into an armchair that was clearly her favorite spot. A nearby side table held a crossword puzzle book, a yellow pencil, a small manual sharpener, and a coaster adorned with birds. "Addison said you had some questions for me."

Since she'd been out of town, I asked if she'd heard about J.B.'s murder.

She had not.

I told her what had happened at the reception, how the police suspected Lena Quinn from the library, and how I'd been quietly looking into the matter. At last, I brought the conversation around to my main question. "I heard that for many years, your family has given a large scholarship to a local high school senior. About twenty years ago, wasn't J.B. Hodges the recipient?"

"He was," Madge said, the soft wrinkles in her face turning down into a frown. "How sad that someone has killed him."

"When you listed your house with Vanessa Moran, did you by any chance talk about that scholarship?"

"We did indeed. We actually talked about J.B. for quite a while," she said. "I wondered if she might be interested in him romantically."

"Actually, I think she may have been the person who killed him."

Madge's eyes widened. "Vanessa?"

"Not only had he recently been bad-mouthing her real estate business, but the year they were eligible, he beat her out for that scholarship."

"I had no idea," Madge said. "Each year, my parents and I reviewed three applicants put forth by the nominating committee, but the names were removed, replaced by a number. We were only given the name of the winner once we'd chosen."

"From what Kate remembers, Vanessa wanted to be a stockbroker, and that scholarship was the only way she could afford to go to college. Because of her parents' financial situation, she was afraid to take out student loans."

Madge had turned pale. "She wanted to be a stockbroker?" Her voice shook.

"She did. I guess real estate was the closest she could do without a degree. I know it seems odd that she'd kill J.B. after all these years, but there are other clues that point to her."

"It doesn't seem odd at all." Madge held a hand to her collarbone. "I can't believe I didn't see it. What day did the murder happen?"

"May 28th."

"Oh, my gracious." Madge clutched a hand to her heart. "It was all my fault. I left town and had no idea."

"Your fault?"

"When Vanessa and I talked, I told her that J.B. ended up being a shoo-in for the scholarship. That there was one other strong candidate, someone who wanted to become a stockbroker, but that the nominating committee told my parents and me that an unsigned note said that—unknown to the teachers—that student cheated on almost every test. I had no idea the person we eliminated was Vanessa."

I stared at Madge in silence.

"Two days after I told her that," she said, "J.B. was killed."

A knot formed in my stomach. "If that note was a lie—"

"And if she thought J.B. wrote it..." Madge's voice faltered.

"Then it makes a lot more sense that the events of twenty years ago led to the murder a week and a half ago. Because she just learned the truth about what happened," I said. "It wasn't only that he beat her out for a scholarship or that he recently bad-mouthed her real estate business. If she just learned he unfairly won that scholarship, that could have been the trigger."

Madge sank back in her chair and wrapped her arms around herself. "My father wanted to be sure the award was given to someone truly worthy. He hated the thought that someone might have cheated in school. If that person was innocent, and the winner lied to get the scholarship..." She looked away. "I'm glad Daddy's not alive to see this."

A large grandfather clock struck a three-note melody.

I glanced up. "It's a quarter to three? I've got to run. Check-in starts in fifteen." I stood and then looked back at Madge, shrunken into her chair. "Are you—are you going to be all right?"

"I'll be fine, dear." She slowly got to her feet. "I've weathered worse shocks than this, but what are we going to do about Vanessa?"

"I'll call Cal Granger as soon as I get to the inn," I said. "It's not just the conversation you had with her. There are other clues that point to Vanessa. I'll tell him the whole story."

"I'll be available if he wants to talk to me." Madge

pressed her lips together and sighed. "My parents thought they were doing such a good thing with that scholarship."

"I'm sorry," I said. "Even though this is distressing, you have to know that over the years, your family helped a lot of students."

She gave a small nod but didn't seem convinced.

I didn't know what else to say. I wished her well with her move and tried to cheer her by repeating what Lena had said about her prospects for bridge victories at the retirement community, but I could tell it didn't help.

If I'd been in her position, I'd have been horrified too.

Her family's good deed had inadvertently led to murder.

The sooner I told Cal, the sooner Vanessa would be behind bars, and the sooner Claremont would be safe.

Chapter Twenty-Two

A GOLD SUV with Oklahoma license plates was parked in front of the inn when I returned.

Drat. I'd gotten back with two minutes to spare, but there were guests waiting to check in.

With no time to park in my normal spot by the kitchen door, I pulled in next to the SUV and raced in through the front.

A couple in their forties immediately rose from chairs near the check-in desk. "Do you work here?" the man asked. His dark mustache twitched.

"I'm Meredith Whitfield, the owner of the inn. I'm so sorry you had to wait. Let me get you checked in." I dropped my purse behind the desk and pulled up the reservations screen.

"Is our room ready?" he asked, a note of irritation in his voice.

"Your room is definitely ready," I said. "And I apologize again. I had to run out for a moment."

"Not your fault," the woman said. "We did see on your website what time check-in began, and we knew we got here before that." She pushed back her hair and shot a pointed glance at her husband, who looked back at her, tension still radiating off him.

Once I showed them the map with the hiking trails around the lake, explained about the discount they could get at the marina as guests of the inn, and suggested dinner options, even he looked happy.

I gave them their keys and offered to help with luggage.

They assured me they could easily handle their bags and headed up the stairs.

As soon as they were gone, Tater appeared in the door from the library and hopped onto the reception desk.

"You could have been charming them until I got here," I said to him.

He gave me a look of disdain and wandered away. Apparently, a cat had better things to do than entertain guests.

I checked the computer, learned the names of the two other guests who would be checking in, and then my phone rang from my purse. I dug it out. The call was from Madge.

I clicked the button to connect the call and held the phone to my ear. "Hello?"

"Meredith, I brought in my mail right before you arrived, and I spent a long while looking at the 'For Sale' sign in my yard." She exhaled audibly. "It's hard, you know, thinking about leaving this place."

"I can only imagine." I wasn't quite sure where she was going with this.

"Anyway, I just noticed that the For Sale sign has a new banner on it that says, 'Open House This Sunday.' That banner wasn't there before you came over. This may seem paranoid, but what if Vanessa had stopped by while you were here? If she saw your car, would she recognize it, suspect what we were discussing, and know you were onto her?"

I pictured the back of my car, which advertised not only my love of the Kansas City Royals and Chiefs, but also my new Roseview Inn bumper sticker. My stomach tightened. "Yeah, she would definitely recognize my car."

Suddenly, the front door of the inn opened.

Madge said something, but I didn't hear it.

Because Vanessa stood in the doorway, light glinting off her fair hair, pointing a gun at me.

"Hang up the phone." Her jaw was rigid. "And don't bother screaming, or I'll shoot you and be out the door."

The air thinned as if the oxygen had been removed.

My mind raced faster and faster, like a rabbit chased by a dog, searching for safety.

Suddenly, I had one tiny, desperate idea. "Uh, hey, Lena, you know that recipe I said I was going to make as soon as I got back to the inn?" My voice sounded oddly thin as I spoke into the phone. "Could you, uh, could you make that for me?"

"Lena? Recipe?" Madge replied. "You didn't say anything about making a recipe as soon as you got back. You said as soon as you got back you were going to call— Hold on. Are you in danger? Do you need me to get ahold of Cal Granger?"

She understood! "Yes," I said quickly.

"Hang up now," Vanessa commanded as she stepped closer.

"That would be wonderful. I know they need that cake right away. Thank you," I said, hoping Vanessa hadn't over-heard Madge's voice and recognized it.

No need to put the older woman at risk.

I was in enough trouble all by myself.

My fingers shook as I disconnected the call.

"You couldn't let this go, could you, Meredith?" Vanes-sa's voice was brittle. "And don't play dumb. I know you know that I killed J.B. I'm sure you put it together after you talked to Madge. I'll take care of you, then her."

My breath grew so shallow I could barely get air.

I should never have gotten involved, never continued when Cal told me to stop, never have endangered Madge. And now...

I stood frozen, straining to hear if there were footsteps moving about above me, if any of the guests were coming downstairs. For the moment, I heard nothing. But if one of them did ... I couldn't bear to think about it.

My only hope was that Madge would call the police, and they would get here in time to prevent another killing.

That would only work if I could keep Vanessa talking.

"You don't need to hurt Madge," I said. "I figured it out, but I didn't tell her. No need to make her feel bad about what her family did." If only, I thought, I'd been that smart.

Vanessa looked at me with disgust. "She was as much a part of it as her parents were. She could have told them not to take a scholarship away from a worthy recipient based on an anonymous rumor."

"It *was* only a rumor, wasn't it?" My voice was wobbly, but I had to stall, and this seemed like it might work. As angry as she was, maybe she'd welcome the chance to tell her side of things. "You never cheated, did you?"

"Not once." She stood taller. "I worked my butt off in high school, thinking that if you played by the rules, you got rewarded. I just knew I'd get that full-ride scholarship, get a degree in finance, and make my family proud. I'd help my parents get out of debt, and I'd be a success."

"Then the nominating committee got that note," I said. "Do you think J.B. sent it?"

"Think?" She snorted. "I know he did. Who else would have had a reason to? We both knew we were the only real contenders for the award that year."

"That does make sense."

"At the time, of course, I simply thought the Pullmans had picked him. It stung, but I was so young and foolish I believed it had all been handled fairly. I didn't get the scholarship, didn't get to go to college, but I found a way to make a success of myself anyway."

"You really did."

"Darn right." Her jaw tightened. "I had to work day and

night though. I scrambled and begged and did anything I had to in order to get those early listings. And I never had the prestige or income I could have made if I'd gone into finance."

"You've built an impressive reputation as a real estate agent," I said.

"J.B. even tried to ruin that," she spat out. "What a worm of a man."

"What he did was wrong," I said.

"But I put up with it. I kept my cool. Until I learned about how he sabotaged my application for the scholarship back in high school. That was the final straw."

I nodded, trying to look sympathetic. "And Rita?"

"Rita?" Vanessa's voice turned flat, and her eyes narrowed. "Enough talk."

Oh, why hadn't I let her continue talking about the past? Apparently, once the sympathy for what she'd suffered in high school was over, so was our conversation.

She gestured with the gun toward the library door. "We're heading out the side door and over to Lookout Point, Meredith. Unfortunately, the loose gravel up there can be slippery and, well, as the new owner of the inn, you should have put up a fence. It might have prevented the tragic accident that led to your death."

My pulse pounded in my head so hard that I could barely focus, barely think.

Maybe, as we walked through the library, I'd find a weapon, but what would that be? A throw pillow? An extra-large book?

She jerked the gun in a hurry-up gesture, and I slowly walked around the reception desk.

As I passed Tater perched on the desk, I stroked the soft orange fur between his ears. My heart constricted as I silently told him goodbye.

The moment I came from behind the desk, Vanessa stepped behind me and shoved the gun into my back. "Move it."

Chapter Twenty-Three

My chest felt tighter with every step, and I walked toward the library as slowly as I could, hoping against hope that—

The front door banged open, and Vanessa and I both spun around.

"Drop the gun, Vanessa!" Cal Granger shouted.

For a second she hesitated.

Then she let out a high-pitched wail and dashed past me, out the side door.

My knees gave out, and I sank to the floor as Cal raced by.

A moment later, an officer ran into the library. She helped me up, walked with me to a couch, and brought me a glass of water.

Tater peeked out from under a nearby chair and, after sniffing her feet, jumped up on the couch beside me and nuzzled my arm.

I pulled him onto my lap and held him close.

The officer stepped to the window and then turned to face me. "They've got her in handcuffs."

Ten minutes later, Cal Granger sat in a chair across from me and looked at me. "Are you okay?"

I sat up taller. "I am. I'm just grateful Madge understood what I meant when I talked about a recipe."

"She understood exactly," he said.

"Thank goodness." I guessed bidding in bridge was basically talking in code. If anyone would have understood, it would have been Madge. If she hadn't ... I pictured the drop from Lookout Point and shuddered.

"I'm taking Vanessa into the station." He gestured toward the front parking lot. "Officer Baker here will talk with you a while longer, and I need you to come by tomorrow and make a formal statement, okay?"

"I will."

"And from now on, no more sleuthing. You nearly got yourself killed." He shook his head, then stood and walked away.

I sank back against the couch.

The next evening, after I'd closed the front desk for the day, Kate, Addison, Philip, and I gathered around the staff fire pit in the Adirondack chairs.

The sun had dipped below the horizon, leaving a hazy swirl of orange and purple and pink that reflected in the surface of the lake. The soft calls of insects and frogs heralded the evening, and the warm air carried a faint hint of wild honeysuckle.

A fire might be cozy in the fall, but for now, simply sitting out here together was as comforting as anything I could imagine. Especially when Kate passed around a plastic storage container filled with chocolate crinkle cookies that were left over from afternoon tea.

The cookies—rich chocolate, covered in powdered sugar—had the perfect chewy texture, and soon the storage container was empty.

Addison scratched the base of Tater's ears, making him purr so loudly that I could hear him from the other side of the fire pit.

And I sat there, my heart at peace, processing all that had happened. Had it been less than a month since I'd arrived at the inn, still in shock over my inheritance? Such a small amount of time on the calendar, but it had been long enough for me to make three new friends and, with their help, solve a murder.

For a moment, we were all silent, as if taking a collective breath.

"I'm glad it's over, but I'm still bummed about what happened," Addison said eventually. "You inherit the inn and then there's a murder here. It's got to make you wonder about Claremont."

"Really," Kate added. "It's a good place."

"I can see that," I said. "Every community has some people who cause problems. Except for Vanessa, the folks here might not be perfect, but at heart, they're good people. And Claremont has an interconnectedness, a sense of community, a charm that's unique."

Addison, Kate, and even Philip nodded.

"I saw Cal at the post office today," Kate said. "From what he told me, a lot of the clues that made us suspect various people were planted by Vanessa."

"He told me the same thing when I went in to make my statement," I said. "Like how she learned Elliot was struggling to make his mortgage payments—a private matter that certainly isn't a crime—and spread it all over town."

"I don't think Elliot will struggle much longer," Addison said. "I heard he handled a big sale for Cal's mom. Some collector in California bought a dozen of her latest works at a premium price."

"Holy cow!" I blinked. "Good for Cal's mom, and good for Elliot."

"Vanessa was also the reason we suspected Shannon," Kate said. "She got Candace Wells to tell you about how J.B. bought that lakefront property, and she used coffee to make the threatening note smell like the coffee shop in the bookstore."

"The coffee part didn't work. I didn't connect it with Shannon." Deep down, had I known she was innocent? "I connected hazelnut coffee with Elliot. Turns out, the fact that he loves it was only a coincidence."

"I'm glad Shannon is innocent," Addison said. "I really like her."

"I do too," I said. "I think what she did with the tomatoes was one out-of-character action, not who she really is." Despite that one action, she was a nice person, a person I could see becoming a good friend. She'd even stopped by earlier in the day with a stack of books she thought I'd enjoy, hugged me, and said I needed something to take my mind off my horrible experience with Vanessa.

"Vanessa's position in real estate gave her access to sensitive information—information she used to manipulate us," Philip said.

"She used it to manipulate the police as well," Kate added. "Cal said they wasted time investigating some of the same lies we did."

"What about Tony?" Addison asked. "He really did sabotage that big dinner reservation, didn't he?"

"He did," I said.

"He always has been kind of a hothead," Kate added.

And yet, he'd called the inn the previous day as soon as he heard about Vanessa pulling a gun on me. He'd wanted to make sure I was okay, and he'd made me promise that if I ever felt unsafe at night alone in the inn, I'd call the police immediately. "You're new to this business," he'd said. "I tell all my employees—male and female—that being in the hospitality business does not mean you should put yourself at risk."

Underneath, he might be a pretty sensitive guy. How much, I wondered, of his arrogance was nothing but bluster? "Although what he did with that anniversary reservation was wrong, I bet his wife's cheating hurt him a lot more than he let on."

Everyone nodded.

"How is Rita doing?" Philip asked.

"Much better," Addison said. "I stopped by to see her this afternoon. She still doesn't remember the day of the attack, but everything else has come back to her." She gestured to Kate and me. "The day you two first tried to talk to her at the gift shop, before her doctor's appointment, she had run into Vanessa at the bank. Something in their conversation made Rita suspicious."

"Interesting," Kate said. "Why was she so slow returning to work?"

"The doctor's office was backed up, but she really wasn't that late returning to the shop. The clerk just wanted her back so she could leave early for a date. She's apparently not been the best employee. She and Rita had agreed that it wasn't a good fit, and she should look for a new job."

"If Rita was suspicious of Vanessa, why didn't she tell the police?" Philip asked.

"She felt uncomfortable accusing someone of murder based only on her gut feeling," Addison said.

I could have told her that a person should always trust their gut. "So where did she go the next day on her day off?"

"She drove to a town on the other side of Bellamy Lake to see a friend whose sister is a cop," Addison said. "After Rita got back to Claremont, she planned to go to the police. On the way home, though, she had car trouble in an area with no cell service. She spent the rest of the day walking to get help, then taking her car in. The next day she had interviews all morning to try to hire a new clerk. When she finally got those done, she had her phone out, ready to call the police. That's the last thing she remembers."

"Oh, wow," Kate said.

"Rita's daughter, Kimberly, thinks Vanessa must have picked up on the fact that Rita suspected her at the bank," Addison explained.

"Then she sneaked into the store and hit her over the head right before we got there." I shook my head. If we'd gotten there a few minutes earlier, Rita might have been spared.

"Rita's lucky to be alive," Addison said. "Now that it's all over, I can't believe I ever suspected her. She was upset by how J.B. had treated her daughter, but she never acted on her anger."

"I guess a murder in a community makes you wonder about a lot of people." I sat up taller. "On the plus side, it has also shown me what good friends I've made here."

I looked from Kate to Addison to Philip, filled with gratitude that each of them had come into my life. And Tater took that moment to wander up and nuzzle my leg, purring so loudly he snorted.

I scooped him up—using both hands, since he was such a big boy—and settled him into my lap.

"It has been an exciting few weeks." I mulled my decision one last time and slowly nodded. "I admit, when a murder took place at that reception, it gave me pause. When you talked about an event at the Roseview Inn that no one would ever forget, Kate, murder was the furthest thing from my mind."

"Mine as well," Kate agreed. "Mine as well."

"When I came here," I said, "I gave myself thirty days to decide if I'd stay. But now I … I think I will."

"Yahoo!" Kate leapt to her feet and pulled Addison out of her chair. The two of them danced around the chairs circling the fire pit in a conga line singing, "She's staying, she's staying."

"Oh, you guys." I laughed and waved them back to their chairs. "I don't know for sure that this is my future, but the chance has been given to me." The role of innkeeper might be a good one for me, especially with the way I liked caring for people. "I know I'll have to work to make the inn financially stable, and I'm not sure I can achieve that, but I'll try."

"That's all we could ever hope for," Kate said.

"Not only because we believe that together we can make the inn a success," Addison said, "but also because we love working with you. You wouldn't believe all the texts we've sent back and forth the past few weeks, analyzing every comment you made, trying to figure out if you'd stay."

Emotion welled up in my chest, clogging the back of my throat. I'd known it had been a major decision for me, but I'd had no idea it mattered so much to them. "Thank you," I said softly.

My two best friends in Kansas City had moved away, leaving me feeling lost, but that loss had been part of the reason I'd decided to give the inn a try and found new friends. I guess that just showed that life couldn't be predicted, that it always held surprises.

Philip reached over and brushed my shoulder. "I'm also

glad you're staying, Meredith." His gaze was warm, with a hint of something more than friendship. "After all, we need to find that valuable item Jasper hid."

"You don't still believe that, do you?" Kate asked. "If the story was true, someone would have found it decades ago."

I caught Philip's eye. "You never know. I found the secret storage space under the stairs."

"And that letter about a hidden room," Philip added.

"Who knows what else we might find?" I smiled at the three of them. My eyes lingered on Philip, and I felt an odd flutter in my chest, half-startling, half-pleasant.

There were possibilities here, maybe even possibilities I thought were all in my past.

"In the meantime," I said, "I've still got a lot to learn about running an inn."

Epilogue

OUTSIDE THE INN, a bolt of lightning split the sky, and rain began to pelt down.

Grateful to be inside, I turned back to the new guest I was checking in, a woman named Annabeth Langley, and smiled. "Glad you made it before that started."

"Me too," she said.

"Here's your key." I handed it to her. "You're in Room 6."

"Thank you." She slid the key into her pocket, and the large rose-shaped enamel pendant of her necklace caught the light.

"I can't help but notice your necklace," I said, leaning forward to get a better look. "It's lovely."

"Thank you." Annabeth, who appeared to be in her late sixties, beamed at me, her eyes shining. "I'm an artist. I made this in honor of my grandmother. I was inspired by a pair of earrings she had."

"I guess I've become fond of roses myself lately. I recently inherited the inn."

"How exciting." She glanced around. "What a fantastic property to inherit."

"It is. It's changed my whole life."

At that moment, Tater hopped up on the reception desk and approached us.

"I also inherited this fellow. His name is Tater." I rubbed the velvety fur between his ears.

He strolled over to Annabeth and, after peeking up at her until she said hello to him, nuzzled her arm.

"Wow," I said. "He's taken to you so fast. Normally it takes him a while to warm up to a new guest." From what Kate and Addison had told me, the only other person he'd taken to so quickly was me.

"He certainly is a handsome fellow," Annabeth said, scratching him under the chin.

"He is," I agreed. "And he can be a real comfort, more than I ever imagined." My heart warmed as I gazed at him. I hadn't realized how much I'd needed a pet, but Tater had been good for me. He might sometimes be a little silly, but he was always affectionate, always sweet, pretty much a fuzzy ball of love.

In his own way, he'd even helped us figure out who killed J.B. Hodges. If he hadn't been such a soothing presence, I might not have ever relaxed enough to see what made Vanessa look suspicious.

Annabeth ran a hand down Tater's back, then turned toward the stairs, refusing my help with her single bag.

She'd barely stepped away, though, when a beeping sound came from outside.

A second later, a young man entered the front door. "Meredith Whitfield?"

"That's me."

"We've got your mattresses and box springs. The right size this time—kings."

"Wonderful," I exclaimed, then turned to Annabeth. "We're making some upgrades."

"Sounds smart," she said. She headed up the stairs with Tater following behind her.

I signed the paperwork and led the delivery men up to the first room we were redoing with the king-size beds. Kate and Addison were both gone, but I texted them and they replied, thrilled to hear the news.

As the delivery men unwrapped the mattress and rested it atop the box spring, tingles ran down my arms. The king-size bed fit the room perfectly. The padded headboard, with its Victorian curves, had arrived earlier in the week and helped maintain the feel of the room. The inn might not be quite as historically accurate as it had been when Mrs. Everly ran it, but with luck, we could strike the right blend of historical serenity, elegance, and pampering.

These new mattresses were a significant step in our plan to revitalize the inn, to possibly one day make the Roseview Inn a destination resort that was booked year-round.

In the process, I might learn for sure if I'd found the right direction for my life.

I wasn't certain we could make a go of things financially, but I thought we just might.

I'd left a lot behind back in Kansas City—memories of my dear husband, Clint, my children's childhoods, and my friends. Eventually, I would have found a new job there, built new friendships, and gone on with my comfortable routine.

Here, though, I'd found new friends and new challenges. I'd found my sweet, fuzzy companion, Tater. I'd even found out I was not too bad at solving crimes.

Maybe, just maybe, this change was exactly what I needed.

Tomorrow there would be beds to make, laundry to wash, a million details to juggle, and—just possibly—a new clue about what Jasper had hidden.

Thank you for reading this story!

Are you ready to return to the Roseview Inn? Continue Meredith's journey in the next mystery, ***Marina Misdirection,*** or read the prequel, ***Innside Incident,*** to discover how she first met Kate, Addison, and Tater.

Marina Misdirection

A summer celebration. A vanished host. A body adrift.

Meredith Whitfield is finally finding her rhythm as innkeeper of the Roseview Inn. Between flaky biscuits, fluffy towels, and flurries of summer guests, she even manages to enjoy a lakeside Fourth of July fireworks show —until festivity gives way to fear.

When the local marina owner steps away mid-celebration and never returns, Meredith and her friends grow concerned. But the real shock comes the next morning: the woman's body is found floating in a small boat, strangled and set afloat during the booming distraction of the fireworks.

Suspicion soon falls on the small circle of guests invited to the dock that night—including Meredith's own friends.

Armed with her intuition, a supportive sleuth team, and one very cuddly cat, Meredith must untangle a web of secrets—before the killer vanishes like smoke over the water.

If you like a cozy mystery with small-town connections, found family, a hint of romance, and a lovable pet, you'll love Marina Misdirection.

Don't miss your free cozy mystery bonuses!

Join Sally's newsletter to:

• Receive the Roseview Inn prequel, ***Innside Incident***—free!

• Enjoy exclusive bonus material and behind-the-scenes extras

• Be the first to hear about special announcements and new releases

Visit https://sallybayless.com/roseview-prequel to join the fun!

Love small-town sleuths? Visit Dogwood Springs for another cozy series filled with secrets, twisty mysteries, friendship … and four furry paws.

From time to time, Sally also shares bonus Dogwood Springs content with her newsletter subscribers.

Acknowledgments

Big thanks to you, dear reader, for joining me in this new series. I can't tell you how much I appreciate your support!

In addition, I'd like to thank all those helped me behind the scenes. Taking this book from initial idea to finished product would be impossible to do alone. I am so grateful to everyone who helped me with *Hot Tub Homicide*. If, in spite of the efforts of all these people, errors snuck in, they are mine alone.

Thank you to:

My beta readers—Betsy Anderson, Debbie Edwards, Barbara Hackel, Janice Huwe, Martha Long, Carrie Saunders, and Stephanie Smith. I am so grateful for your early comments on the story. You made it so much better!

Robert A. Holm, Jr., D.O. FACEP—for so kindly answering my medical questions.

My author friends—Ana Bisset, Cathryn Brown, Lou Collins, Kelly Brakenhoff, Brook Peterson, Stella Bixby, and Della Pearl. I can't tell you how much I appreciate your encouragement as I dove into this new series.

My editors—Thank you to Lori Fairchild for her developmental editing wisdom and to Tegan Maher of Magical

Words Editing for dealing with tricky grammar and style issues and for spotting those sneaky inconsistencies.

My cover designer—Donna Lynn Rogers of DLR Cover Design. I love what you have done with this series!

My wonderful family—Dave, Michael, and Laurel. Thank you so much for your support!

About the Author

After many years away, Sally Bayless lives in her hometown in the Missouri Ozarks. She's married and has two grown children. When not working on her next book, she enjoys reading, BBC mysteries, word puzzles, swimming, and shopping for cute shoes.